SYSTEMA PARADOXA

ACCOUNTS OF CRYPTOZOOLOGICAL IMPORT

VOLUME 29
MAD DOGS & ENGLISHMEN
A TALE OF THE BARGHEST

AS ACCOUNTED BY ALAN SMALE

NEOPARADOXA
Pennsville, NJ
2026

PUBLISHED BY
NeoParadoxa
A division of eSpec Books
PO Box 242
Pennsville, NJ 08070
www.especbooks.com

ISBN: 978-1-956463-93-4
ISBN (ebook): 978-1-956463-92-7

Interior Design: Danielle McPhail
www.sidhenadaire.com

Cover Art: JW Harp
Cover Design: Mike and Danielle McPhail, McP Digital Graphics
Interior Illustration: JW Harp

Copyediting: Greg Schauer and John L. French

Dedication

For all the Good Dogs, and their owners.

Especially Chip, the dog I grew up with, a black-and-white border collie who was kind and affectionate and thus very different from the canines (and many of the humans) herein.

And for my parents, Peter and Jill Smale, who bought me Chip in the first place, and also helped to ignite my lifelong interest in British history and folklore.

Chapter One

The great beast opened his eyes and saw nothing. Sucked a long breath deep into his aching lungs and smelled only dampness, limestone, and his own dank and dirty fur.

Muscles stiff. Bones that ached through to the marrow. And a stomach that was very, very empty.

He shifted his position, and his sinews creaked in protest. He breathed some more, turning his head this way and that, building up a scent map of his surroundings as best he could. A stony cave, constricted and narrow where he lay, but open and high-ceilinged in front of him. As he crawled forward over the cold, uneven rock and leaned his head to the left he felt the faintest of breezes, with hints of new buds and blossoms upon it.

Interesting. The last smells he remembered were of the brown and fallen leaves of autumn, and wood fires, and decay.

The beast licked dry lips and tried to stand, but his legs buckled. He huffed out a brief snort of protest and tried again.

Better, this time. He swayed, tottered a little, but he was up.

One step forward into the darkness, then one more. His hard claws snicked on the limestone floor of the cave, but the way ahead of him seemed level.

The barghest set out, in search of spring.

It could not have been a change in the light that had awoken him, for there was none. Nor could it have been the chill: this far underground the limestone crack he had wedged himself into was a steady, cool temperature all year round. And certainly it was no sound, for the occasional drip of water some distance away in the cave system was all he could hear, besides the occasional thump of his own heart and the blow of his breath.

As that heart began to beat more regularly his body warmed, and as a result he began to shiver, just a little. He dipped his muzzle down toward the floor and smelled the dry soil from his own footprints, made as he had walked into this cave.

However long ago that had been. For all the acuity of his physical senses, especially smell and hearing, the barghest had little sense or understanding of time.

But now the light grew around him, a fuzzy blue and grey, as he approached the mouth of the cave. Here the limestone was slick with rain and the flowing of water, and his claws slipped and skidded, but he did not fall again. He was more alert now, more aware of his surroundings and his balance. He sniffed at the air, identifying many plants, flowers, and insects. The smell of scat, that from the lambs brighter and milder than the dung of adult sheep. His stomach rumbled.

He came out into pale sunlight and blinked.

Today he was a gaunt creature, his shaggy black coat loose around a frame of sinew and bone. His body was dry, almost desiccated. He was still largely moving on instinct, with few glimmers in his mind beyond survival. To survive, he needed to drink. And to eat soon after, to ease the sick, nauseating emptiness within him.

Not trusting his footing now, amid the clumps of grass and wet rock, the barghest crawled forward and dipped his snout into a puddle of water by the stream, lapping at it with his long tongue.

The beast had emerged from the inner wall of a limestone gorge with the trickle of a beck running through it. The barghest spoke no language, but to the men and women of northern Yorkshire who lived in the nearby hamlets of Burnsall and Skyreholme this gorge was known as Trollers Gill, and this intermittently flowing rivulet as Skyreholme Beck.

That is, when they spoke of it at all. Strange stories were told of Trollers Gill. Of actual trolls, who rolled rocks down upon people rash enough to walk through the ravine. And of a giant dog-like apparition that frequented the area with glowing red eyes, claws for paws, and jaws that could effortlessly crunch bone, a fearsome beast that stole cattle and sometimes even humans as its prey, ripping them apart with contemptuous ease.

Such a beast would surely be a terrifying sight, quite unlike the frail skeleton with fur that now lay down to rest and let the sun warm him.

After he had finished panting, he used those jaws to tear at the tough grass around him. Grasses held little nutrition for a natural carnivore, but at least they held moisture. The smell of it rich in his nose, it was natural for him to bite it and pull some of it into his mouth. And the grass helped to sooth a stomach that had fed only on its own juices for… however long it had been.

Eventually he stood again and made his slow and steady way uphill, ever upward onto the moors, for now keeping as far as possible from even the long-distant scent of man. Sheep scattered away from him, repelled by his rancid odor and obvious wildness; sheep with black faces and white shaggy coats, with fleecy lambs trotting away alongside them. They were too stupid to realize that he couldn't even break into a trot, let alone run one of them down. Right now, he would barely have the strength to chew on a lamb if it dropped dead right in front of him.

That would come, with time.

For now, the barghest kept climbing. Ascending, in slow stages, to the top of the peak of Wharfedale millstone grit that humans called Simon's Seat, high ground with a view over the surrounding dales, a place where he could take stock of his surroundings. See what was up, and what was down. Where he had awoken this time, relative to the villages and towns of human beings that posed the only threat to a creature of his size.

The barghest's fate had always been closely aligned to the fates of the men and women around him, although the beast himself understood that only dimly.

And yet he already knew he had awoken for a reason, and that reason was on the wind that whipped through his fur as he climbed.

And the barghest would follow that scent wherever it took him.

Chapter Two

As Lindsey Ambler trudged down from the broad summit of Pen-y-ghent, legs aching and lungs weary, her phone buzzed against her chest. An incoming call. She grinned and ignored it.

Naturally, since this was Yorkshire, a fine misting rain had begun to fall on her. Just enough to make the grass slick underfoot, but not enough to slake her thirst when she stuck her tongue out. "Ha," she said aloud, with what little breath she had to spare. "Nice timing."

She was carrying her phone inside a clear plastic holder at the end of a lanyard that was looped around her neck. After it stopped buzzing at her, she twisted it to look. Jurgen, obviously, and he'd left a voice mail message that Lindsey had no intention of listening to until at least tonight, but possibly never. Two minutes later it rang again. This time she didn't even look down.

The Pennine mountains of Whernside, Ingleborough, and Pen-y-ghent were close together, and collectively known as the Yorkshire Three Peaks. Some hardy souls made it their goal to hike to all three summits in a day, a twenty-four-mile circular route with over five thousand feet of ascent in total. That took twelve hours at a minimum, and in Lindsey's case would likely take much longer, and more leg strength and endurance than she currently possessed. Maybe next year? If she was still here?

For now, she was quite content to conquer them individually. Four days ago she'd ascended Whernside, the highest and arguably easiest of the three, and from its peak she'd been able to see west into the Lake District, clear out to Morecambe Bay and the Irish Sea. Today she'd tamed Pen-y-ghent, though the view at the top had been limited by the clouds. And sometime in the coming fortnight when the weather cleared up and her blisters had scabbed over, she might finish the trio. She'd deliberately left Ingleborough until last; the broad plateau that formed its summit was home to a fifteen-acre Iron Age hill fort, with several hut circles and parts of the defensive wall still visible. It had probably been built by the Brigantes, that Celtic tribe that had rebelled so fiercely against the Roman invaders in the first century AD.

With Lindsey's innate sense of history, Ingleborough felt like the natural climax. After which she'd declare herself "fit," or at least fit enough for a woman in her mid-forties who'd been chained to a desk job for the past twenty years.

No peaks in England were higher than two thousand five hundred feet, but you underestimated them at your peril. With their steep slopes and slippery grasses, treacherous rocks, and occasional peaty bogs, hiking in the Yorkshire Dales and Pennines was always an adventure. Originally Lindsey had shunned trekking poles as being effete and unnecessary, but she'd become a quick convert; having them to lean on during brief rests, using them to thrust off with, and particularly being able to support her weight on them coming down steep slopes. They'd already saved her from several tumbles. Yorkshire in April wasn't for the faint of heart.

The pair she used were nice: adjustable, carbon fiber pole, cork handle. Because Lindsey deserved the best. But that also meant Lindsey didn't have a hand free for her phone… which was probably also for the best.

Bouncing against her chest, her phone pinged. A text, which meant it was probably Marie. When Jurgen couldn't get hold of her, his next move was generally to try to get at her through his secretary, who was another Brit living in Germany.

"Hey phone, read text," she said, in between puffs as she strode down the hill.

The phone's voice was not Marie's, of course, but maybe close enough. "Hello there, lady. Jurgen's having a right meltdown."

Lindsey grinned. She could just imagine that very British phrasing coming out of Marie's mouth. "Hey phone, text Marie. Must be Tuesday, smiley face emoji. Send."

Another ping. "Hey phone, read text."

"Jurgen says, answer your goddamned calls."

To that, Lindsey just shook her head. *Of course* Jurgen wanted her to answer his goddamned calls, and of course she absolutely wasn't going to. Lindsey didn't work for Jurgen anymore. Because he'd fired her three weeks ago, in Munich. And since then, he'd quickly learned just how hard she'd been working on projects critical to the company's success that he hadn't bothered to brief himself on, and how many useful contacts Lindsey had made that had kept those projects running smoothly and the revenue flowing.

So, he'd had second thoughts. Obviously. *Too late, chum.* Way too late. Lindsey was gone gone gone, and she wasn't coming back, and especially not to freaking Munich. She'd never liked Germany, not a bit, not for a single day of the decade she'd spent there. By now she was in a different headspace altogether and enjoying much more congenial surroundings.

Ping. Marie. "Jurgen says he'll bring you back on no questions asked and raise your salary twenty percent, but he needs you to pick up your freaking phone *right now*. Well, he said all that in very bossy German. But, ya know."

Ping. Marie. "He's big mad though, so you should probably wait half an hour."

Ping. Jeez, Marie again? "Uh-oh. He's got smart and is texting you himself now."

Ping. Jurgen. "Really, you are going to make me do this by text?"

Lindsey grinned. Sort of. "Text Jurgen: Why not, all the kids are doing it. Smiley face emoji. Send."

Ping. Jurgen. This one was in German, which the phone made a surprisingly good job of pronouncing. But the gist of it was: "Come back. I need you. Your team needs you. You can't just walk away from all this. Do you have no pride? Listen: twenty-five percent raise and that's my final offer. But you must tell me today, right now. Do you understand?"

Which was rich, since Jurgen had fired half of Lindsey's team the same day he'd fired her. That same team Lindsey herself had put together with her own sweat: a team of smart and funny individuals that had become the only decent part of living in Germany.

"Do I have no pride?" she said out loud, ironically. Because the dude had fired her because of Brexit, and less demand, and market factors, and nothing personal, and he was sure she understood.

Sure. Lindsey understood just fine. And also, yes: Lindsey had her pride.

Ping. Jesus Christ, Jurgen, have *you* no pride? "Deal ends today. Do not come crawling back to me next week. It is today or never..." The word *bitch* just hung in the air, unspoken.

Which was just one more reason Lindsey would never, ever be going back. She wondered how she'd put up with him this long.

Time to end this. She stopped walking and focused on the phone. She wanted to remember this moment. "Text Jurgen: No deal. I'm never coming back. Stop texting me. Get lost. Go die in a fire. Send."

Okay, maybe *die in a fire* was a bit much. Oh, well.

Ping. Jurgen. "Where the hell are you anyway?"

"Text Jurgen: Uh-oh, losing cell signal forever. See ya never. Send," Lindsey said, and turned off the phone.

She took a deep breath and looked around her. She was still in Yorkshire, and it was still beautiful. Maybe even more so.

The heather, yellow gorse, thistles, and clumpy grass of the moorland top were now giving way to the greener, more lush but still scrubby grass of the Dales. Sheep everywhere, *baa*-ing at her. A nice fresh breeze.

She was ready for the next stage in her life. A stage that would not include any of the following: software, Munich, clients, pitch meetings, and especially that fricking ass, Jurgen.

What was that *next stage*? Lindsey was still considering options. Maybe get a small job, part-time, something very different from the big job with big pay but major stress that she'd just left behind. In a shop, in a bank, whatever. Or she could start a consultancy. A simple one, helping people with their laptops. There were always enough computer-clueless people around who'd pay a little bit for installs, advice, troubleshooting. Or maybe she'd write a book. Anything was possible.

And the great thing? She didn't need to decide yet. Lindsey had a reasonable financial cushion. She could just hike the countryside and read books in front of the fire for a *long* time before running short. Cook herself some nice meals or eat some yummy pub lunches followed by terrible British ice cream. And chill out a bit.

One thing was for sure: Lindsey was done with the rat race. She'd traveled abroad enough for the time being. Whatever the Meaning of Life was, or at least the meaning of *her* life, she'd be looking for it here, or hereabouts. Perhaps even in Yorkshire.

And surely a healthy mind in a healthy body was part of that.

Yes, it certainly was a lovely day.

She hadn't been focusing at all on the (very few) people she encountered on the trail, had been deliberately keeping her eyes averted from them, because after all she was the jerk who was hiking and talking on the phone, which Brits looked down on. So she hadn't been paying attention to the young, cheerfully blond guy approaching, hiking up in the opposite direction, with a Jack Russell bounding along by his side. A cheerful, spunky little pooch, the definitive Good Doggo, with brown face and floppy ears, and a patchy brown-and-white body. Kinda cute, if you were into dogs the size of a small cat that yapped like a squeaky door instead of barking like a *real* dog.

Lindsey nodded and smiled at the straw-haired lad and his Good Boy, like you do, and gave them plenty of space… only the Jack Russell gave her a dark look and lunged in like a tiny dog tornado, biting her on the calf just above her boot.

"Christ!" Lindsey kicked upward instinctively, and the tiny Satanic creature flew briefly through the air before landing on all fours and turned to square off against her again.

Seriously?

Lindsey walked straight at it, trekking pole raised. She had no intention of hurting the creature, ridiculously small as it was, but she very much wanted it to *back off* and not bite her again.

"Please, please!" The straw-headed hiker stepped into her path, mortified. "Oh my God, I'm so sorry! He's never done that before! He loves people, he just… are you all right, are you all right? I am so so sorry!"

Of course, Lindsey stopped. Her attention was on the dog, obviously, but the little beast sat back demurely, and showed no signs of coming at her again. Just as well, because she'd have drop-kicked the little runt clear into Wharfedale.

Fine.

"Sure, I'm okay." Was she? She squatted to check out her leg. For all the shock and surprise of it, the nip from Mr. Russell didn't look like it had drawn blood. Punctured the skin, yes; stung like hell, also yes, but she wouldn't mention that. "No worries. I…" She glanced at the Jack Russell again. Now, butter wouldn't melt in its mouth. At least that presumably meant the little beast didn't have rabies. "No harm done. Please don't mention it."

Ah, *please don't mention it*. The most English phrase ever.

"Well. Sorry. Sorry again. Enjoy your day."

"You too."

Lindsey sighed, pushed herself upright, and set off again.

Three hours later, in the early evening, Lindsey wearily walked through the streets of Peasholme, the village where she was renting a cottage. Today had been a bit far after all. Bitten off more than she could chew, perhaps? Fortunately not like that tiny, darned dog with the sharp teeth…

"Uh, ma'am? You're bleeding."

She looked around and, yes, a tall guy a little older than her was frowning and pointing down at her calf.

Sure enough. That bite that she'd thought was superficial had somehow worked itself into a ragged cut, which was now bleeding all over her boot. "Oh, great." She stopped and perched on a wall, pulled out some tissues. "Thanks."

"Is that a *bite*?"

"Yeah. Stupid yappy little dog up on the moors. I'm okay, though—"

"I'm sure you are, but… you know what? Just stay there a sec." The guy looked around, then crossed the road and went into the Boots pharmacy nearby.

Lindsey shook her head and tried to soak up the blood on her boot. That was going to leave a stain. New boots, too.

The chap came back out with antiseptic and a small packet of band-aids. "Here you go. Best to see to it ASAP, right?"

"I suppose," she said. "Uh, ta. How much do I owe you?"

"Oh." He waved it off. "No worries."

He had a definite London accent. Not a local, then. Lindsey swabbed her war wound with the antiseptic as efficiently as she could, hissed at the sting, looked up, and he was still there. "Well, thanks. I'll be fine now. Thank you." Then realized he was the only person she'd spoken to all day aside from the dog's owner. *Getting a bit isolated here, Lindz.*

But that was okay. She didn't really *need* company.

He looked at her uncertainly as she pulled out the largest band-aid from the box and slapped it over the cut. She had the definite feeling that he was itching to be on his way, but he was held back by that ridiculous British solicitousness. A German guy would have pushed off long ago. "You sure you'll be okay?"

"Yes, thanks. All I need is a stiff drink at this point. But," she hurriedly added, "no need to hold you up any longer. You were a big help. Appreciate it." His clipped London way of talking was wearing off on her.

"All right," he said, with obvious relief. "Well, then. I'll be off."

"Okay, then," she said. "Off you pop. Thanks again."

He nodded, and strode away, not looking back.

Lindsey waited until he turned the corner, then looked around for the nearest pub.

As this was England, she didn't have far to go.

Chapter Three

Legend held that the barghest, like the mythical vampire, could not cross running water. Legend was a lie, proven false yet again as the barghest leapt into the River Ouse, fastened his jaws around a small tench and, minutes later, splashed his way to acquire a slightly larger silver bream. He was growing in strength daily and had progressed beyond mice and voles to larger prey. Soon enough, he'd be ready to take on a more impressive challenge and know that he was whole again.

None saw him, and he'd already been soaked through before his accurate leap into the river; rain streaked diagonally out of the sky, blown crossways by a brisk wind. The barghest felt none of it. The layers of fat and muscle under his skin had been building steadily over the past two weeks. And with it, the barghest felt his aggression building too: that inner drive, the coarse rage that defined him. The desire to take on larger prey and take it down, that bloodlust that led him to kill, and kill again, and to rend and dismember and utterly destroy. To feel the hot spray of blood in his mouth, the bellowing of distress from his victim. The harsh joy of the kill.

And so, later that same day, the barghest stared at a bull, and the bull stared right back. Sixty feet separated them.

The bull was a horned Hereford with a rust-brown hide, white face, dewlap, and neck crest, and white socks. Behind its heavy, short neck, its shoulders were broad with muscle and its flanks were solid with meat. Short, thick horns curved down to either side of its head.

Some bulls feared dogs, but this bull certainly didn't seem deterred by the barghest. Malevolence radiated out from it. The bull probably hadn't seen anything quite like the barghest before and may not even have recognized him as a dog's ancestral relative.

The barghest paced left, keeping its eyes firmly on the bull, then stopped and turned and stalked back to the right. Back and forth, savoring the scent of the bull as it lingered on the air.

The bull showed no signs of retreat. It huffed, stamped a front hoof against the ground, and lowered its head.

Little enough reason why the bull should fear him, after all. While neither beast comprehended human units of measurement, the difference in their sizes was stark. The barghest was three feet high at the shoulder, where the bull was over five feet. The bull weighed two thousand three hundred pounds, and the barghest a mere two hundred and fifty. The battle looked… unequal.

And it was.

The barghest was not daunted by the bull's bulk. He, or some dimly remembered previous he, had prevailed against worse. In his dark mental shadows, either recalled directly or passed down through some ancestral memory, the barghest glimpsed an even more giant creature, twice the bull's size and shaggier, and with a snout that extended out from its face like a snake and knew that once in the past he had conquered this trumpeting, gigantic foe, all by himself.

In the barghest's world, it was kill or die. And if he couldn't kill this ruddy, snorting creature, he deserved to die.

His sense of smell already told him this animal lived on grass; its teeth were not made to rend and tear, and so could cause the barghest no harm. Those horns, though? Those could certainly pierce his hide, even drive deep into his chest or throat. Another distant memory, of a goring: long ago, but painful. Those horns deserved respect, but if he was quick enough, the bull wouldn't have time to bring their sharpness and power to bear on him.

Those hooves, with the weight of the bull atop them, could certainly cause him grievous bodily harm. If the bull could stomp the barghest, the battle would be over quickly.

Now the bull pawed at the ground, churning mud rather than kicking up dust. An aggressive male, young and ripe with testosterone. And here it came, charging across the field toward the barghest, its hooves flinging up clods of grass and dirt, narrowing the distance between them with astonishing rapidity for a creature that size. As it approached, the barghest paced to the right, then to the left, and the bull veered its course from side to side to compensate.

A mere thirty feet away, the bull lowered its head, horns down, hard skull to the fore and… the barghest broke into a sprint of its own, straight toward the massive bovine, bellowing in his own strange not-a-wolf roar.

When ten feet separated them, the barghest surged forward and to the right with a startling burst of speed, then swung in toward the bull's flank. But the bull was too fast for him and was also surprisingly agile; it spun almost on a sixpence and lunged, those goring horns at the ready. The snap of the barghest's jaws could have been heard from a hundred yards away, but he had missed the bull's throat and had to leap away.

He darted in again, but once more the bull was too swift, and so the wolf-beast kept going, running around it. He stopped and started, skidding in the mud, swerving forward and leaping back, worrying at the bull and giving the ponderous beast not a moment's peace. Adrenaline surged through his veins, and his blood almost sang. Ferocity filled his thoughts. All he knew was the thrill of the attack, the hot, thick pulse of battle. Even as he danced around the bull, the barghest slavered in anticipation of the kill, and gobs of saliva dripped from his jaws. His teeth itched for the bull's blood, for those feelings of rending and tearing, and the swallowing of warm meat.

Patience best served him, though. This bull was still strong, and younger and quicker than his size would indicate. It would take time to wear him down.

At one point the bull broke away from the combat and lumbered off, but escape was impossible. The barghest could run both faster and for longer. He nonetheless allowed the bull to achieve some distance before he sprinted after it, lunging in to snap at the bull's rear thighs when he could, then springing away to avoid the hooves.

And then the bull turned and leapt over the drystone wall that surrounded its field, its front hooves kicking over only one or two of its topmost rocks.

Well, that was a surprise. Fear had given the bull wings.

The barghest ran in a wide circle, his big claws digging into the wet earth as he built up speed, then easily cleared the wall in a mighty arc that took him ten feet further into this new grassy field before he landed.

The bull stood before him, panting. Winded, with big gouts of steam rising from its mouth, it eyed him balefully.

The barghest trotted around the bull, huffing to regain his own breath. The bull turned, keeping horns-first toward the predator as best it could, but its strength was clearly broken.

Now, with victory in sight, the barghest succumbed to a vicious playfulness, surging in toward the bull and breaking away, twisting and turning. Rearing up onto his hind legs as if to stride in, then dropping forward. The initial roar of attack had given way to low growls now, throbbing and resonant from the depths of his chest, a terrible and sinister sound.

It was a good five minutes more before the barghest's hunger overcame his sadistic sense of play and he swooped in for the kill. The bull raised its horns one last time, but fatigue dulled its reactions, and when the barghest ducked under and struck, the bull was too slow by half.

The barghest's jaws sank into the bull's throat and tore it out. Blood and gore spattered the grass around him. The bull toppled onto its knees in pain and tried to raise itself again and rake at the barghest's chest and shoulders. But there was no strength behind this last, despairing attack, and the barghest easily twisted away. The bull's horn merely scraped against his coat, almost skipping across the sleek black fur, not even drawing blood.

Even as the horn slid off his body, the barghest leapt up to land on the bull's back and sink those terrible jaws into the bull's crest. One rending bite, then another great bound to throw himself clear in case the bull were to fall and roll on him.

Indeed, the bull fell onto its side, and with an almost leisurely air, the barghest walked in to deal a final wide bone-pulverizing bite that destroyed what was left of the bull's throat and chest.

Next he tore into the area between the bull's ribs and its rump, where he knew the juiciest and tastiest meat would be and was not disappointed.

As the barghest feasted, his eyes at last began to glow coal-red.

Chapter Four

The Wise Owl turned out to be an English pub in the classic style: lots of deep red leather, shiny gold glinting on dark wood, and old countryside scenes in too-large picture frames. Stools along the bar, and high-back wooden chairs around tables, several of which were still free.

She saw a couple of men here and there, and a family sitting by themselves tucked into a corner, but Lindsey's eyes skipped across all those, looking for the women, and found them.

A youngish woman was working on her laptop, a pint of Theakston's in front of her. Another woman a little older than Lindsey sat in a corner, her fingers busy on her phone and a folder of papers and half a lager in front of her. Okay, so this was a place people came after work, and where "people" didn't just mean men. A pub for friends, and for singles, as well as groups.

Which was just the ticket. No one would hassle her here.

She dumped her rucksack on an empty chair at a table by the window and limped up to the bar. The young chap behind it hustled over to her, drying his hands on a tea-towel. "What'll it be?"

"Gin and tonic, please."

He scanned her briefly. "Double?"

"That obvious?" she said.

"Have a seat," he said. "I'll bring it over."

Not the usual British pub etiquette—unlike German beer halls, they didn't do table service in the UK unless you were eating—but she'd take it. "Thanks," she said in heartfelt relief, "chuck a slice of lime in it if you've got one, yeah?" And went over to her table to slump down next to her pack.

Lindsey wasn't a beer drinker even before Munich, and definitely not afterward, and in fact was rather fond of French aperitifs and cocktails, but she wasn't about to order a Cosmopolitan or a Negroni in a down-home Yorkshire pub. Besides, the pungency of the gin and tart bite of the tonic went well together. It tasted like the wind off the Dales, like the slight acid prickle of some of the Yorkshire folk. It was a forthright drink, the perfect icy Yorkshire adult beverage… provided the pub actually had ice, which many didn't. This one, fortunately, did.

She pulled her tablet and keyboard out of her rucksack and set them up, took a sip of the G & T when it arrived, and started tip-tapping on the keys, typing the day's impressions into her journal file. Around her, the pub began to fill up, the noise level rising.

And then the guy from the street, the one who'd bought her the band-aids and antiseptic, walked in and stepped up to the bar. Was he looking for her, deliberately trying to find her again? Well, probably not. But maybe.

Boy, Marie really does have me feeling paranoid.

He bought his drink and turned. Naturally his gaze met hers almost immediately, and he did a double-take that looked genuine. "Oh. Hello."

"Hi," she said, and blushed. Of all the stupid things. She transferred her attention back to her tablet screen.

He looked around. There were still a couple of seats at the bar, but he didn't look like the sitting-at-the-bar type. He swallowed and turned to her again. "Um. This chair taken?" He didn't even wait for her to hesitate. "Not gonna bother you, scout's honor. You're obviously busy." He drew a line across his lips. "Mum's the word."

"Uh." Lindsey would rather have preserved her own space, but the pub was getting busy, and if not him, who knew who might show up next? Better to fill that seat with a known quantity. Well. Partly-known. A Good Samaritan type, anyhow.

Lindsey waved noncommittally. "No. I mean, sure. Help yourself."

"Thanks." He gave a bob that was almost a small bow. Sitting down with his pint, he studied her face for a moment, then looked away, giving a good impression of a man surveying his surroundings. He took another sip of his beer and cleared his throat.

Here it comes, she thought. *Any second now. The just-making-conversation moment.* She frowned a little more intently at her tablet and started typing again.

But he was as good as his word. After a few moments he pulled a book out of his jacket and started to read it, paying her no attention at all.

A book, and not his phone. Well. That was almost refreshing. She resisted the urge to sneak a peek at what he was reading, Turning her attention back to her journal, she clattered away at the keys a little more.

Twenty minutes later. "Uh, sorry. But: guard my seat?" He held up his empty glass. "Need to see a man about a dog, then get this filled up."

"A *dog*?" Oh, right. Bathroom break. "Uh, sure. Go ahead."

"Ta."

A few minutes later he came back with his next pint and put a gin and tonic down beside her.

Lindsey frowned. "Um. I…"

"No worries. Call it rent, for a seat at the table." He picked up his book and began to read again, ignoring her completely.

The crowd at the bar was now two deep, and what was she going to do? Go buy herself her own drink while the single ice cube in this one melted?

"Thanks, then," she said. She sipped it, then typed for a while longer.

If this was a pickup attempt, it was the slowest and most patient effort she'd ever encountered. And, this was clearly ridiculous.

Lindsey picked up her phone casually, opened an app and pretended to scroll, then checked to make sure the flash was off and covertly snapped a picture of him. She'd silenced the stupid fake shutter sound long ago, so he had no indication of what she'd done. Then she texted the picture to Marie. *Six feet, maybe five eleven. Broad shoulders, cropped salt-and-pepper hair. London accent. Kent? Essex? Jeans, flannel shirt. Maybe fifty years old? In the Wise Owl, Peasholme, Yorkshire, England, The World.*

Three dots began dancing in the app as Marie typed back. *oh yeah, who dat?*

Guy I'm about to introduce myself to.

for reals? what happened to lone wolf lindsey? i dont need a man lindsey?

Lindsey snorted, sipped her drink, typed some more with her thumbs. *Still don't. Don't even fancy him. Just a chat. You made me swear I'd be careful, no? To tell you All the Things, no?*

*okay then girlfriend have a good c*h*a*t and I'll check in with you tmrw morning lol lol.*

The three dots appeared again—more Marie-snark incoming—but Lindsey put the phone face down, took a big pull at her latest G & T, and did that long surveying-the-pub move that he'd done when he'd first sat down. A comfortable hubbub was growing. The businesswoman doing her accounts had been replaced by three young men and a woman, all with pints in their hands, talking animatedly. She and Band-Aid Man here were the only people in the entire place not engaged in conversation.

At that moment, he glanced up at her.

She indicated his glass. "My round. What's your poison?"

He stared at the glass for a moment, as if considering. "Sam Smith's." He glanced at his watch. "Just a half. Getting toward my bedtime, but why not? Thanks."

"Watch my stuff, yeah?"

He mock-saluted her. "Will do, ma'am."

Three gins in a night. Lindsey was living it up. Well, English pub measures were wicked small, right?

She made it back safely with a half pint of bitter in one hand, a Bombay Sapphire and tonic in the other, and two bags of cheese and onion crisps gripped between her ring finger and little finger. "To soak up all this nonsense," she said as she dropped them onto the table.

He raised his eyebrows and poured the half into his pint glass, setting the empty aside. No straight British male liked to be seen drinking from a half-pint glass. "Well, cheers."

"Cheers," she said, and took a swing of gin. "Lindsey."

"Roger," he said, which she took for a name rather than an acknowledgment, and they chinked glasses. After a pause, he said "Roger Cane."

"So," she said. "What brings you here, Roger Cane?"

He seemed to be thinking. Coming to a decision, he looked around the pub again before eventually replying: "I'm in hotels."

Lindsey blinked. "Well, sure. Me too, sometimes."

"No, I mean I work for a hotel chain." Cane glanced around again. It almost seemed like a nervous tic, for him. "We're scoping out the North for a bit of an expansion, figuring out what's what. It's all rather hush-hush, really, if you don't mind; we don't want the word to get out."

Lindsey nodded. "Because half the punters would be all keen and want the extra business a bunch of swish new hotels would bring, and the other half would be wanting your guts for garters for Over-Developing the Quaint North."

He raised his eyebrows, but also looked wary. "You're in the business?"

"No. Computer systems analyst. Mostly software sales. I've just seen how this goes. People aren't fond of change. Especially British people." He gave her a quizzical look at the qualifier, and she added, "I've spent the last ten years in Germany."

"Ah, I see. My condolences." Cane took another long pull at his beer and looked around. "Like this whole area hasn't already changed dramatically in the last twenty years since I was up here last. Cutesy little tea shops. Souvenirs. Flowerbeds and flowerpots everywhere. Just driving through Leeds, Sheffield, even Bradford, it's obvious there's a lot more cash around than there used to be."

"So, you're just visiting, then?"

"Extended visit. Driving around the area. Getting out and about. But also spending way too much time sitting in meetings in other hotels, looking at revenue projections and artists impressions and, well, basically just watching PowerPoint charts go by."

"Oh God, tell me about it." Lindsey raised her glass. "To the eternal damnation of PowerPoint."

He chinked her again. "So. You're not in Germany now, I see?"

"Fired," she said. "Smallish British-owned so-called-multinational based in Germany? Brexit was killing us, and my boss decided that axing me would help his bottom line."

"Oh, sorry."

"No worries. His loss. And it was a great excuse to get the hell out of Munich." She made an effort not to slip into the mad anti-Brexit or anti-Munich rants she'd given twenty times before, and instead waved her hand around. "I'm originally from here, anyway. Not the Dales, but Leeds, so close enough. Thought I'd come back to my roots for a bit, while I'm figuring out my next move."

"Okay." He eyed her carefully. "I voted Remain, for what it's worth."

"Oh, me too. Obviously. Remain all the way. But, hey, let's just shoot ourselves in the foot as a nation, why not?"

"Right," he said, with a wry look.

Before she knew it they were off and running, into what turned out to be quite a nice chat, and a pub dinner and a couple more rounds, school night or not.

Leaving the pub two hours later, Lindsey walked a couple hundred yards down the street with her head down before stopping abruptly and looking back over her shoulder to suss out whatever might be happening in her wake.

Or whoever.

A whole lot of nothing, as it turned out. Two girls in short skirts, arm in arm. Group of likely lads in their twenties going the other way, loudly joshing each other, who'd probably had a couple of pints too many and paid Lindsey not the slightest attention. A few other solo guys out and about, generally older, walking fast in different directions with their heads forward, in that typical determined Yorkshire Dales somewhere-to-be and Christ-that-wind-is-brisk sort of way. A short, slender blonde woman, maybe in her thirties, on the other side of the street, going the same direction as Lindsey but busy typing on her phone. The woman glanced up at her, gave her a preoccupied nod, and went back to her screen.

So, no. No one was paying particular attention to Lindsey.

More to the point, Cane wasn't following her.

Well, good. Lindsey hadn't really thought he would—the guy honestly didn't seem the predatory type—but she'd have hated to think her creep radar sucked *that* badly.

They'd parted with straightforward platitudes, nice to meet you, good luck with the hotels, enjoy your new life in the Dales, all very innocuous. No plans made to meet again, or even suggested. No phone numbers, no complications, no awkwardness. Just a casual chat in a pub.

No perturbations to Lindsey's new me-myself-I regime. She needed to focus on getting her life together right now. Besides, the guy would probably be in Harrogate or Skipton by this time next week, or Northumbria, or wherever, bringing affordable hotel accommodations to the masses.

If anything, she sensed that he'd been more wary of her than she of him. Even once they'd started talking it had taken a while for that tension to unwind. Roger Cane was clearly cautious, at best.

No reason apparent. If Cane had been in bad relationships in the past, he hadn't mentioned any. And he wore no wedding ring, nor did he have grooves or a band of lighter skin on that finger that would indicate that he'd recently taken one off.

And already I'm overthinking this. Jeez, Lindz, get a grip.

After all, he'd made no attempt to get any of her personal information. He hadn't even asked her surname or the name of the company she'd worked for. Hadn't offered to walk her home. He'd just looked at his watch as if surprised to see the time when the barman had called last orders, said his goodbyes, and gone off on his way. Several other people left at the same time; tomorrow was a workday for many, meaning tonight wasn't one for carousing.

Anyway. It was a nice night, and it was good to be up and around again, stretching out those weary leg muscles. She'd text Marie once she got home to head the innuendo off at the pass. And after that, she would definitely need her bed.

Peasholme, the village Lindsey had chosen as her base, was pretty without being twee. It had been mentioned in the Domesday Book as a farming outpost, and presumably had been occupied ever since, so it had a thick strand of continuity, combined with a largely unknowable history, and Lindsey found that attractive. It possessed the quaintness that came from age, but it wasn't stuck in the 1970s like some Dales villages. Peasholme had a solidity that had survived the strong and biting gales of Yorkshire, the march of time, and the occasional war. And it was situated in a valley that was typical Dales country, surrounded by drystone walls and sheep, field barns and rolling hillsides, reaching up to the moors on the mountains around. Granite chunks spilled out of the sod on those hillsides, geology just breaking out of the ground all around her. Her parents would have called the terrain bleak, or maybe barren. Lindsey did not see it that way at all.

The village center she was currently walking through was a maze of twisty streets not meant for cars, even though cars did pass gingerly through on a dubious and confusing one-way system. Lindsey herself didn't own a car: too expensive, nowhere to park it, and no need for one anyway. She'd sold her left-hand-drive Volkswagen when she'd left Munich, and the British trains and a surprisingly efficient public bus service were doing a fine job of getting her wherever she needed to go. She could be self-sufficient here anyway: the village had a Tesco Express and a Budgens, both glorified convenience stores but with enough fruit and vegetables for her to get by, plus bakeries and butchers and coffee shops. On the nights when she didn't feel like cooking there was pub food, plus two fish and chip shops, a curry house, and an incongruous Thai take-out place. And aside from the estate agents, outdoor stores (camping, climbing, cycling, hiking, adventure!), and a half-reasonable bookshop, that was about it, setting aside a couple of souvenir shops and purveyors of premium sheepskin and cowhide rugs for the tourist trade.

And, of course, it was safe for a single woman to walk around, despite Marie's over-protective conniption fits, even though Lindsey's house was well away from the main street, on the edge of the country-side.

In a village full of quaint houses, Hazel Cottage had to be one of the quaintest. Its outside walls were all original Yorkshire sandstone, tight-grained and a deep grey-blue, that glistened in the infrequent sunlight with traces of quartz and mica. Its windows were mostly small and mullioned, aside from a much more modern picture window looking out over the Scarsdale valley. Inside, it had been renovated where it really mattered, and left alone where it didn't. From the small front hallway area you could walk forward into the kitchen or turn right into the combined lounge and dining room area. Stairs to the upper floor were on the right as well. The kitchen had been renovated in the last five years; the cupboards and cooker were all new, and the fridge/freezer and washing machine were a respectable size, but there was no dishwasher. In the lounge, the wood-burning stove in the fireplace was new, and so were the hardwood floors.

Upstairs, the renovations were a work in progress. A small master bedroom with a super-king bed rather painfully shoehorned in, plus an adjacent twin bedroom that could only have been used by one person, or siblings who really liked each other. One bathroom, quite small, with a shower that clunked indignantly whenever it was turned on and muttered to itself for a while before disgorging a thin trail of hot water, poised precariously over a clawfoot tub. The sink was of old vitreous china, apparently built for an age when men and women were much shorter, with a mirror mounted on the wall directly opposite the window, so that during the day all she could really see in the mirror was her silhouette. Per the landlord, the upstairs renovations were a project for a future year. Inconvenient, but it meant the rent was only half the price of the five-star holiday cottages that were spreading across the villages and hamlets of the Yorkshire Dales. That, and being here well off-peak, had given Lindsey quite a bit of bargaining leeway.

She'd signed a six-month lease, with an option to extend. She hadn't yet decided whether she was up to the rigors of a Yorkshire winter, but if so, the rent then would be even cheaper. Maybe she'd be writing her book by then and be happy to sit home scribbling during the long winter nights. Or getting her web site up to snuff. Or whatever.

Out front it had a little garden the size of a postage stamp, mostly lawn with a small border of sage and mint, some primroses, and a rhododendron bush, all bordered with a comically small brick wall, low enough to step over, obviously just for show. Beyond was a nice view of the valley, outlined with drystone walls and studded with stone barns and other small farm buildings. Often the first sound she heard in the morning was the *baa*-ing of sheep.

It was charming, but not backward. Lindsey was still living in the twenty-first century: the heating and WiFi in the cottage worked flawlessly.

So this was the cozy sanctuary that she was walking toward, skimming the news on her phone, when she glanced up again to look across those fields, and froze.

Out in the darkness, something was watching her. A dark form with glowing red eyes. "What?"

Could that really be an animal? Or moonlight reflecting off something? Or…

As she watched, the twin red coals vanished and quickly reappeared, all in a fraction of a second. She knew she hadn't imagined that. The creature had just blinked.

Then, just as her own eyes were adjusting to the dark again, whatever it was—that amorphous black shape against a black background—turned and… disappeared completely?

For some reason, she thought again of the Jack Russell, sinking its teeth into her calf, and felt a twinge from that area under its neat band-aid.

She set off walking again, much more briskly, and didn't stop until she closed her front door, locked it, and turned the lights on.

The snug familiar rooms of Hazel Cottage had never looked so welcoming.

Had she really just seen some weird creature at a distance? Was it just her imagination, or the gin? A bit of both, maybe? Anyway, her heart rate slowly returned to normal.

Even if whatever she'd seen had been real, it had been a long way away, and hadn't approached her or threatened her in any way. Still, for a moment there it had been a little unnerving.

"God," she said out loud. "What a day."

Maybe tomorrow would be better.

She glanced up at the bottle of Glenfiddich on the top shelf of her kitchen cupboard. A nightcap? No, she'd had enough, and she didn't want to mix whisky with the gins she'd already had.

"Hey, phone," Lindsey said. "Text Marie: home safe and alone, thank you very much. Off to bed now. Sleepy-head emoji. Send."

Chapter Five

1650 AD

The barghest had been to this city before, this collection of men all living together cheek by jowl in their own filth. The city that humans called "York" advertised itself to him from many miles distant. The fetid smell of the rotting corpses hanging from the three-legged gallows at Tyburn on the Knavesmire, at the boundary of the city, a reek that fought for dominance with the stink of the tanneries along the river's edge outside the city walls. And above both of those, the miasma of odors: human sweat, middens crammed with rubbish, and the excreta of men and beasts.

When York came into view, the barghest's eyes could perceive it only dimly. It was dominated by the solid, chunky shape of York Minster, the great cathedral, flanked irregularly by the slimmer spires of the more common-or-garden parish churches. But soon enough, he arrived at the bank of the river that humans called the Ouse, which he would follow into the city.

On closer approach, the barghest could now distinguish the subtler smells of the brewhouses and bakeries, with their complementary and excessive odors of yeast and malt. More distracting than those, even: York was a market city, with livestock pens just outside the walls. With reluctance, the barghest gave these a wide berth. No good came of attempting to kill and feed there.

The medieval city walls were substantial, with barbicans fortifying the gates. Yet, taking the river route, the barghest easily passed into the city without being seen.

Yet more smells, now, and much more directional: garbage again, the mingled smell of innumerable unwashed human bodies, each of whom now stood out as distinct individuals to the barghest's astonishing powers of smell, half a million times more sensitive than the human nose.

And overlaid on the people-smells, a myriad of other aromas: tobacco and snuff, wine and butter, coal smoke and candlewax, and some scents new to him since his last journeys into the towns and cities of Man: coffee and chocolate and fatty cocoa, the former almost making him sneeze with its pungency, and the dark sickly-sweet tang of the latter two exciting him in a way that distracted and confused him until he learned how to filter them out and disregard them.

The smells formed a three-dimensional pattern, a scent map of the entire city. And yet, within that map, the barghest rarely lost lock on that one particular human scent that he was tracking, that he had tracked from far across the moors.

With a sense different from his nose but processed similarly within his brain, the barghest was keenly aware of human mortality. Several men and women in the houses he skulked by would die soon; mostly unavoidable deaths due to sickness or malevolence beyond the power of the barghest to alter.

For a human of a scent line he was drawn to, the barghest's instinct might compel him to lie across the doorway of their home. He lacked the awareness to fathom *why* he felt such a compulsion, but compelled he was. Fortunately, the number of people alive right now who owned one of his favored scent lines was vanishingly small, and today he was not distracted by them. None of them would die, not tomorrow or within a few days at least, and so he was able to continue through the dark and dirty streets of York, wending his way along narrow alleys between ramshackle Tudor buildings that still survived, slinking along roads and lanes all unseen. People were abroad, many for nefarious purposes, but this was late evening and the barghest's shaggy coat was night-dark. The shadows absorbed him almost entirely. His head he kept lowered, partly to sniff at the ground before him, and partly because he understood that humans could see the glow of his eyes that he sometimes glimpsed himself in his reflection.

Few did. A woman, standing in her regular spot in a doorway awaiting custom, froze in place as the barghest skulked by. Two men, hurrying home from a tavern three streets on, clubs in their hands for self-defense, turned to look at the glint of red, and yet it faded away even as their gaze arrived on their target.

The barghest was adept at concealing his passage, and only dimly aware that at times his form faded away almost to invisibility. It was not a talent that he consciously invoked, merely an adaptive process that had developed over the years and centuries. It just happened, without any volition on his part.

Three men crept through the streets a little ahead of him, and those three were similarly following a fourth man who was completely unaware of their presence. This fourth man was from outside York, from out of town. He was scared and out of his depth.

Steadily, the barghest closed in on the little group. And yet the barghest could not act, not yet. That drive to fight had not yet mounted to the peak where it was impossible to resist. The barghest bided his time, padding quietly through the dark streets, following one frightened man, while shadowing those three predators reeking of their own greed and bloodlust, likewise waiting for the right moment to take their action.

The three men broke into a trot, the leader howling more like a wolf than a human being as the trio of thugs closed in on their victim…

Chapter Six

The man who called himself Roger Cane walked out the front door of his anonymous backstreet bed and breakfast with a confident stride. His head was still a little foggy after last night's beers, but his senses were on full alert. He glanced up and down the street but saw only a few people walking away on business of their own. No one ducked back into cover, no one seemed to pay him any heed. He looked next at the cars parked along the kerb, but none of them had anyone sitting behind the wheel. No one with a camera, no one taking notes, and he recognized most of the cars from previous days. Cane had a pretty good memory, especially when his life was at stake.

With barely a pause he set off, heading for a coffee shop on the village's main street but taking the long way around. He varied his route every day, as well as his departure time and destination—there were certainly enough cafés in this sleepy village that he could keep up an uneven cadence. Unpredictability, that was the key.

He'd set false trails, natch. Bought plane tickets to Barcelona, Prague, and Athens, none of which he'd used, plus a rail ticket to Paris through the Channel Tunnel. He'd already parked a car registered in one of his false names in a Heathrow lot and left it there, presumably forever; and parked his other car in his real name on an anonymous Dover street. Laid credit card trails in two other directions down into Europe. He had to hope that was enough, and that the Drakens wouldn't have men out trawling half-dead villages throughout the north of England for him.

Of course, "Roger Cane" looked completely different now. He even walked differently. He'd dyed his brown hair black and wore new clothes of a similar shade. On those rare occasions when he struck up a conversation with anyone, he assumed an affable personality that was only partly his own.

With luck, all this cloak-and-dagger stuff would buy him enough time that the Drakens would get bored and move on.

2020s London wasn't like the gangland London of the 1960s. No Kray brothers. Fewer psychos and wide boys. British organized crime had taken a few steps upward from that. By now it was less about territory—who gave a toss about *streets*? The true power came from *sources*. Making big money these days was less about protection rackets and dockside violence, and more about contacts and communications.

Particularly contacts with large amounts of drugs, who you could trust to follow through on the deal. The Columbians, in South America. The Galicians in Spain. Because, for-fricking-sure: these days drug trafficking was where it was at. Street drugs. Heroin from Afghanistan. Opioids in pill form, particularly the synthetic opioids like fentanyl and the nitazenes. Cocaine, of course, lots of that for the politicians and bankers and stock market speculators. Molly, aka Ecstasy, aka MDMA, for the kids who wanted to dance all night. And methamphetamines for the old-schoolers.

And Cane was into all of that, at least from the distribution aspect. He didn't use any of them himself, of course. That was a mug's game. He even went sparing on the alcohol. Usually. Though, last night? Maybe a few more extra added halves of bitters than he should have indulged in. He'd need to make sure to look sharp today.

He turned the corner and bumped into someone. "Oh, hey," she said. "Small world."

The first thing Cane saw was the newspaper she was holding—an actual, paper newspaper, the classic London gang way of concealing a machete or zombie knife, even a pistol… He raised his arm to shove her away and buy himself the seconds needed to whip out his own knife but recognized her just in time and instead opened his fist to steady her. "Oh, goodness, I'm so sorry. Not looking where I'm going. Hi again, uh, Lindsey."

She had a queer, uncertain look on her face. "Are you all right?"

"Course. Just wool-gathering. Bit of a heavy head, after last night."

Last night, in the pub with Lindsey. Cane hadn't had his coffee yet, but he should be quicker off the ball than *this*.

At least he hadn't stabbed her. Last thing he needed was to start leaving a trail of corpses behind him. That would have put the Drakens back on his tail in no time flat.

An elderly lady with a poodle stepped into the road to get around them, tutting, which gave Cane the opportunity to glance around again. Lindsey was watching the dog warily—once bitten, twice shy—but no one else was paying them any attention.

He popped that easy grin onto his face. "Guess we're blocking traffic. I was just going for a coffee. Fancy one?"

They'd be looking for him, alone, a single guy. This Lindsey might make useful cover.

"Okay," she said readily enough, but she was chewing her lip, he now saw. Something was bothering her. Not the poodle, surely? Seriously?

He took a moment to breathe. Hotels. That's what he'd told her. Not his best idea. It was a cover line that worked well enough in London, where he knew the hotel scene. Not so good here.

Well, fine. He'd show interest in her instead, rather than talking about himself. Women always liked that.

Possibly a mistake. Lindsey seemed obsessed with some other dog she'd half-seen the previous night in the shadows, walking home. She couldn't even tell what breed it was, though. Mostly, what she'd seen was its eyes.

"Maybe it was just a couple of kids vaping," he said. "Those e-things glow, right?"

She shook her head. "I know how e-cigarettes look. These were too bright, and too steady."

"The houses here are pretty close together. There aren't many alleyways for such a big dog to hide in."

"It was out in the fields," she said. "My cottage is on the edge of town."

That took him aback. "You have a whole house?"

"Yes. Leased it for six months, with the option to extend." Lindsey tried a grin. "I'm almost like a permanent resident here. Putting down roots, at least shallow ones. Now I'm wondering whether that was such a terrific idea."

"It'll be fine," he said. "Two weeks from now you'll have forgotten this… dog thing ever happened." Compared to the shitstorm Cane was facing if the Draken warboys found out where he was, Lindsey's skittishness about a couple of eyes in the dark seemed like a serious over-reaction. "If you're worried, why not move into a B&B for a couple of days? I could give you a recommendation." Not for the one he was staying in now, of course. One of those ones he'd already spent a couple of nights in and then moved out of.

Lindsey raised her eyebrows. "You're staying in a B&B? Not a hotel?"

"Yeah, why?"

"No reason. I just assumed."

Oh, right. He'd slipped again. Damn it. "Well, there aren't any of my chain up here, not within an easy drive. That's why I'm here. And I don't like giving money to the competition."

Lindsey nodded. Cane couldn't tell whether she was convinced, or whether she was calmly racking up the holes in his story.

Was she going to be a problem? He really hoped not.

He finished his bacon sandwich and steered her back onto the safer topics: travel, politics, sport. And at the end, since she still seemed unduly preoccupied, he offered her his mobile number, just in case she found herself in trouble. She was such a scaredy-cat that he thought she'd refuse, but she'd calmly pulled out her phone and entered it without comment.

Cane's was a burner phone anyway. He'd would be dumping it at the end of the week and buying a new one. Necessary precaution.

He couldn't get too comfortable, and he couldn't keep making mistakes. If he was to stay alive, Roger Cane needed to stay sharp.

Chapter Seven

That evening, after cooking an easy dinner, Lindsey poured herself another glass of wine, an English sparkling rosé. Another change since she'd left the UK: they now grew wine grapes in Hampshire, Sussex, and Kent. Winemaking in England was an odd silver lining to climate change. Even odder: the wine didn't suck. The sparkling wines, champagne-style, were actually quite good.

She stared at the bubbles rising in her glass for a few moments longer. Then she opened her laptop and typed "Animals with red eyes in the dark" into her search engine.

Because she'd seen it again tonight, in the dusk, away over the fields. Just for a moment. But it had definitely been closer, this time.

Her first thought had been a lynx, or a bobcat. But there weren't any of those left in England, right?

Right. And no bears, either.

She started skimming web sites.

Deer eyes showed up white at night. Badgers: same. Cats large and small, from cougars to house cats: pretty much always yellow-gold through green. Domestic dogs and horses: blue. Foxes: green.

Animals with red eye shine included: coyotes, rabbits, rodents, opossums, racoons, owls, wolves, and black bears. And of that list, England only had rabbits, some ratty little rodents, and owls.

Out loud, she read: "Pupil shape: predators have vertically elongated pupils, while prey animals usually have horizontal pupils."

The glowing red coals from her mystery beast had seemed vertically elongated to her, even from that distance. Okay, not even a rabbit then, unless it was a rabbit that had suddenly turned maneater and started stalking humans.

Wouldn't that be a thing?

Well, yeah, sure it would, but that wasn't what Lindsey had seen, unless the rabbit was more than three feet tall or floating up in the air somehow.

There just weren't any super-duper apex predators in freaking Yorkshire.

She kept looking. More red eyes: alligators, vampires, and Bigfoot. Yeah, this search was going *great*.

Were dog eyes really always blue? She searched some more. No, sometimes they were yellowish-green. It was all about the reflective layer in the back of their eyes…

So, terrific. Lindsey had seen a psycho rabbit, or a wolf or bear, neither indigenous, that had escaped from the zoo. Or the famous British alligator, leaping in the air. Or Bigfoot, sitting down… As her thoughts whirled, she continued to scroll.

BARGHEST.

Lindsey stared at her laptop. The graphic image was terrifying. A giant dog-like creature with a shaggy black coat, big claws where a dog's paws would be, and those massive red, glowing eyes. But most chilling were its big, bone-crunching jaws.

She drew a shuddering breath. Just an artist's impression, of course, straight out of his lurid imagination. Because in the real world, barghests didn't exist.

But Lindsey's fingers danced over the keyboard of their own accord. Her fascination drew her in. Her inner historian was intrigued.

What sort of word was *barghest* anyway? Old English? Norse? Opinions differed. In Old English, "guest" was how "ghost" was pronounced, and the word for "town" was "burh." Hence, *burh-ghest* would equal "town-ghost." Or if the Germans were somehow involved, it could derive from Bar-geist, "bear-ghost", or Berg-geist, "mountain ghost". Sometimes spelled "barguest". Except, why would Germans be naming a British mythical creature? Yet another possibility: the "bar" somehow derived from "barrow," since these mad black dog-beasts were traditionally associated with those tumuli, ancient burial mounds. Bronze age. Anglo-Saxon.

Good grief. Whatever. But these critters had been around for a while, then. They must be real experts at hiding. Like the Loch Ness Monster and, sure, Bigfoot.

Except that Lindsey had *not* somehow seen a mythical beast. A freaking *cryptid*? Nah. That was bonkers.

She typed some more, then sat back.

Well, if she *had* seen a barghest she wouldn't be the first. Not by a long chalk. It turned out there had been a lot of barghest sightings, and sightings of similar giant dog-monsters, all over the UK, through the centuries.

"So maybe not so good at hiding?" she said out loud.

It had to be time for another glass of wine, because this was getting rad.

I mean, this isn't impossible. Right? Lindsey thought. If these beasts were, okay, *pretty* good at hiding, *very* good at not getting themselves shot or captured, and didn't leave their corpses anywhere obvious when they died? And even if they did, perhaps those skeletons might be taken for a super large dog, a bear, or whatever. Some missing link from millennia ago, perhaps.

Okay, what about that? She tip-tap-typed on the keyboard again.

Oh, hello: a prehistoric creature, from the era of gigantic mammals: EPICYON in Latin, meaning literally "more than a dog." In this case, a dog with bone-crushing jaws, a member of the Borophaginae sub-family of canids, which was its own separate evolutionary path. Except that this bone-crushing subfamily had been extinct for five million years, so Lindsey obviously hadn't seen one of *those*.

She glanced uncertainly at her glass of wine. Maybe wine wasn't strong enough for this kind of speculation.

Or, just maybe, she'd already had enough. Sitting alone and half-drunk in this dimly lit cottage with only banging water pipes to break the silence? No wonder she was spooking herself. Maybe it was time to cork the rosé, put it back in the fridge, and read something more light-hearted before bedtime.

And, being rational for just a moment: whatever it was that was lurking outside her house, it had had its chance to attack her, if it was going to, right?

Unless it just hadn't been particularly hungry at the time.

Come on, Lindz. This was all just her fevered imagination, and a lot to be reading into a couple of glowing coals in the night.

Whatever. But as Lindsey turned out the lights and climbed the stairs, she feared she wasn't about to sleep well.

The barghest did not know his own history, of course. But he had mental glimmers of it.

Was there a single barghest, or many? Just one, or a whole ancestral line? The barghest himself certainly didn't know.

He had his memories, his images from the past. Those mental images existed as ghostly pictures in his head: glimpses of places once known, humans encountered, battles fought. Indistinct memories of fights won and lost: stinging reminders of injuries, vicious strikes that sliced clear through to the bone. And yet, among all those patchwork images of fights to the death and deep wounds, the barghest recalled no serious maimings or permanent disfigurements. No death throes, no ebbing of life, no final torment as he breathed his last gasp, or the spray and gush of blood from his jugular as it stole his life away. And also no memories of himself as a cub, a kit, a juvenile, smaller than he was now.

With his limited awareness of self, the barghest had not pondered the existential questions. He could not wonder whether he was one creature or many; whether he had lived for ten thousand years, or a hundred years, or even ten. He had no inkling whether his ghostly memories were his own, or somehow passed down through his sires, or his dams, or through the ether. Like any living creature, his memories sometimes guided him and sometimes thwarted him, could alternately aid or deter him. He knew what he knew, but had no concept of *how* he knew it.

And yet: he did have the faint impression that some of his thoughts were from a very long time ago, from far back in time, many days and nights and sleeps ago. Some memories were harder to reach than others. The memories from yesterday, or the last time he prowled the moors, he recognized as more recent. The more different the world in his memories, the more divergent the behavior of the human animals, the farther back they were likely to be. As humans changed and evolved, the barghest's experiences and memories also progressed.

The barghest himself had also changed. He had not always been the creature he was today. More recently, he could look into a human face and intuit some of the emotions behind it. Usually terror, to be sure, if the human had seen him, but in those times when the human had not, the barghest could still read their faces.

It had not always been this way. He also had memories of human faces that he had not been able to read at the time. Along with actions by humans that had surprised him, perhaps an act of kindness where he was expecting fear or hostility, or an attack when he had intuited that the human was not concerned with his presence — such things did happen, especially long ago. But when those images flitted into his mind, the barghest of today recognized the signs in the facial expression, in the movement of the human body, and instinctively knew he would act differently. Now, he could see signs that the barghest that had undergone those experiences had not been alert to. His understanding of humans had evolved over the years.

And, aside from humans, there were the Others.

Other monstrous dog-like creatures, beasts that smelled similar to the way the barghest smelled himself, but subtly different. Those other creatures were usually black, always large, often ferocious, but occasionally tender. And they all played favorites among humankind too, based on their scent and their history.

The Padfoot, of the area that a human would call Wakefield, South Yorkshire.

The Gytrash, from further north.

The Skriker, from over the Pennines out Lancashire way, that emitted piercing shrieks rather than the respectable bark or roar common to the barghest and others of his kin.

The Gwyllgi and Cwn Annwn, beasts of Wales.

Black Shuck, in southern England, and then off west to the savage beasts of Exmoor and Bodmin Moor, way across in the West Country.

All of these Others the barghest had encountered, if only by scent, from his occasional restless wanderings. But they had their own territories, and unless it was for mating, the barghest did not trespass upon them for long.

Next day, mid-morning, Cane's mobile rang, displaying a number he didn't know. He blinked at it for a moment, then picked it up and went to the window of his boarding house. Without disturbing the net curtains, he glanced up and down the street. Saw no one.

He pushed the button. "Hello?"

"Hi," she said. "Lindsey Ambler."

Ambler, he noted. It was the first time she'd said her surname. "Oh, hi there. What can I do for you?"

"So, well… the weather doesn't look too terrific today, so I'll be stuck at home, and I'm tired of cooking just for myself. Getting a bit bored. Wondered if you fancy coming round for dinner tonight?"

Cane's immediate instinct was to refuse. *No complications.* But… Lindsey seemed okay, and wouldn't it be healthier to make a friend or two?

Then again, the more he talked to any one person, the more chance his cover would slip. And this would be the third time he'd seen Lindsey in a few days. If that wasn't a complication, what was?

Since he hadn't answered right away, Lindsey started to babble in embarrassment: no commitment, she wasn't hitting on him, just two strangers in town, just dinner.

Talking of boredom, Cane was surely getting tired of his own company. So he gave in and said yes, and immediately wondered whether that had been the right answer.

"We outsiders need to stick together," she said. She could probably detect his reticence.

"That we do." He paused. "Listen, Lindsey: I'm happy for the invitation, and I'll certainly come. But just as a PSA, you should be careful about inviting men you don't really know into your home."

"Oh, now you sound just like Marie."

"Sister?" he hazarded. "Friend?"

"Friend. A coworker of mine in Germany. She's always worried I'm ten seconds away from being attacked. We stay in close touch." Lindsey hesitated. "Well. This conversation went sideways in a hurry."

"Sorry," he said. "My fault. I didn't mean to make this awkward. You can trust me."

And she could, a hundred percent. Cane was no threat to Lindsey Ambler. If anything, it was the other way around. Cane felt oddly protective toward her. Lindsey projected a strange blend of gung-ho confidence and naivety, completely self-assured one moment and worrying about glimmers in the darkness the next, super careful about not giving anything away a few days ago and now apparently willing to tell him her address.

He didn't feel romantically inclined toward her. He did feel like she needed someone like him to make sure she was all right. All decent women did. This was a shit world, and bad stuff happened to good people.

So, sure. He would go for dinner, and make sure the bogeyman didn't get her. And it would be a home-cooked meal, off the village's radar. People in small towns did like to gossip.

It would be a touch of normalcy in Cane's weird and, let's face it, lonely situation.

"You can keep Marie on speed dial all through dinner if you want," he said. "So. Where do I find you, and what time?"

CHAPTER EIGHT

There are seven hundred thousand Ford Transit vans in the United Kingdom, and most of them—over sixty percent—are painted a flat white. They are the vehicle of choice for plumbers, grocers, and handymen of all kinds, along with that beloved British archetype, the Man with a Van: slip him a few quid in cash money, and he'll transport just about anything for you, just about anywhere.

As a result, white Transits are effectively invisible. Which makes them ideal for crooks of all types who prefer to travel unnoticed.

In the late afternoon a Ford Transit van, standard white, pulled into the big car park behind the Three-Legged Mare public house in York. Ten minutes later another van, the twin of the first, arrived in the same lot and parked four spaces away. Not a huge coincidence. Nothing to see here.

A nondescript man got out of the first van, slammed the door, and pulled out a cigarette, glancing around to subtly case the car park. A chap with his bird drove in and parked across the way while he was getting his ciggie alight, and when they got out, they paid him no attention. The man watched the tick-tock of the girl's bum under her tight skirt as she linked arms with her date and walked into the pub, nattering away in an over-bright and perky way that made him feel sorry for the guy.

Mark Draken liked his birds either quieter or noisier. Keeping their mouths shut and doing what they were told or crying out in pain: either of those worked better for him than the barrage of casual conversation.

Anyway, Ms. Motormouth was safely inside the pub now and not his problem, and no one else was around to pay him any mind, so Draken stretched his arms over his head, as if he'd been driving for a while and needed to work the kinks out.

As this was the expected signal, the other warboys got out: the second driver, one each from the passenger doors, and two each out of the back doors of the vans. Eight of them in total, including Draken himself, though one of his "boys" was actually a woman, but she was just as hard-bitten and dangerous as the guys. Draken didn't fancy her, wouldn't even have scoped out her bum walking into a pub, but he had a healthy respect for her sadism.

So, seven actual *guy* guys. Draken himself, who'd be carrying a handgun and a blade. The gun was for emergencies only: he liked to keep his wetwork up-close and personal. Briggs was the real gun nut, he'd blast away with his shotgun until the cows came home, Draken figured it was compensation for Briggs being a bit on the short side. Extended his reach, as you might say, but Draken would try to rein him in tonight by putting him outside on watch. Atkinson often packed a blade but favored a cricket bat in a fight. You could carry it anywhere with plausible deniability — "What, this, a weapon? Nah, just planning a bit of a knockabout later with me mates" — but whacking someone with a bat could do a surprising amount of damage, especially to knees, elbows, and fingers. As it happened, Atkinson was also pretty good with it on the cricket field. He was the only one of them who wasn't piss-poor at playing a sport, as opposed to going to Arsenal football matches so they could get hammered on cans of whisky and ginger and then blood some of the opposing team's supporters afterward. Next there was O'Connor, still on the lam long-term from whatever havoc he'd wrought on the British security services in Northern Ireland back in the day. Hammers were really his thing, up close, but he could also wire a decent nail bomb and even fire a gun when needed.

Okay, so those were the warboys in Draken's van. The four in the other van? Fletcher, a bit short on grey matter, not the sharpest tool in the shed but reliable to a fault. Greta, no surname please, who notoriously preferred breaking men to making out with them. Clearly some backstory there that Draken didn't need or want to know. Next up: Boyle, a standard bouncer-minder-enforcer type, large and solid. And finally Thomas, which was his surname, first name Dave, younger than the rest. Davey didn't do a lot of fighting or tormenting, but he didn't need to: he was their technical whizz and gadget guy. Dave Thomas understood how both iPhones and Samsung mobile phones worked, and how to make them talk to each other without the coppers being able to listen in. Also a good wheel-man, his main role tonight would be as lookout and getaway driver.

This was Draken's team. Eight was more than enough to manage a little well-earned vengeance on the man who sometimes called himself Roger Cane, but at least allowed some spare talent to keep watch, run interference, wreck any coppers or bystanders who might come looking too closely, and all that jazz.

Draken wasn't too worried about any of that. This wasn't London, where the coppers knew their shit; this was darkest country-bumble Yorkshire, where no one could find their arse with both hands. The nearest organized crime of any note was in Liverpool and Glasgow. In the whole of Yorkshire, the closest thing to a gang were the skinheads who watched Leeds United play from the Gelderd End at the Elland Road stadium and thought it was a bit spunky to throw a pint glass through a pub window afterward.

This should be a cinch. Grab Cane and break him, killing him slowly. Take a few souvenir photos along the way to pass around the East End pubs, and send a clear message to anyone else who might be considering coming up against the Drakens—that would be Thomas's job, since he could anonymize the header info on the digital files, so they'd be untraceable. After that, back they'd come to York for a few pints and some shuteye in a backstreet flophouse before driving back to the smoke tomorrow in time for dinner.

Piece of piss. But ultraviolent. Easy peasy eyeball squeezy, as you might say.

So. Off into the Dales they'd go, along twisty-turny roads, guided by Greta, who'd been the advance party and knew the lay of the land, to nab Cane and whoever this woman was, this Lindsey Ambler who seemed to be keeping him company.

And then it would be time for some mayhem.

They checked the weapons, went over the plan one last time. Then Draken sniffed, leaned into Fletcher. "You wearing aftershave, bruv?"

Fletcher blinked. "Maybe?"

"*Je*-sus." Draken leaned into the passenger seat of his van, dug into the glove box, and pulled out some wet wipes and tissues. "Here. Get it all off. You think being up north has destroyed Cane's sense of smell?" He watched critically as Fletcher scrubbed at his chin and neck. "You know what? I'm putting you on the outside crew, at least to start. Can't risk it."

"Aw, man," Fletcher complained. "I always get the short straw."

"Yeah, there's a reason for that, you fricking moron." Draken looked around the rest of his squad. "Anyone else wearing aftershave, cologne, or some other crap? Even a bit?" He looked sideways at Greta. "Perfume?"

"Sod off," she said. "Do I look like a slag?"

Draken grinned. "Opinions differ."

"Screw *you*," she said, but without animosity. Draken was the only person in the world who could get away with tweaking Greta like that, but even he was careful not to overdo it. "No perfume, no icky soaps, no scented pads, no nothing."

Draken raised his hands. "Whoa. Too much information. No worries then. So: everyone clear on the drill? Any final questions?"

Atkinson hefted his cricket bat. "Boy, isn't this sucker going to be surprised to see us?"

Briggs nodded. "Best reunion ever."

"For an hour or two, anyway," Draken said. "Until we outlive his welcome."

Everyone laughed except Fletcher, who likely didn't get it. Draken shook his head. "All right, people. Synchronize your watches. Check your beepers. All set? Okay. Then let's go do a bit of home invasion."

Chapter Nine

The doorbell rang and Lindsey went to answer it, checking her watch. If this was Cane, he was an hour early. Had she told him the wrong time? If so, not a problem. The casserole was already in the oven; she just needed to stir-fry some vegetables before dishing it up.

She glanced out of the side window before she opened the door. It wasn't Cane. It was a short blonde woman who seemed vaguely familiar; a moment later, she realized it was the woman she'd passed on the street after her pub night with Cane. Presumably a neighbor, and she was looking worried, glancing up and down the road.

It was raining lightly. Skies were grey. Dusk would be here soon. Should she warn this woman that maybe it wasn't safe out after nightfall because… cryptids?

Or maybe she already knew and was knocking on Lindsey's door for help.

Lindsey unhitched the chain and opened the door. Glancing up the street and across the fields she saw no sign of glowing eyes or the bulk of a semi-mythical creature. No one else around but a guy doing some kind of electrical work on the cables a couple hundred yards down the street, a Ford Transit parked next to him. Nice night for *that*, jeez. "Hi," she said. "Can I help you?"

"Depends." The woman barely spared her a glance. "Do you own a dog? Maybe yay big?"

Her gesture indicated a height a little over three feet. Just what Lindsey had seen out in the wilds. Her stomach lurched, and her eyes darted left and right.

Play it cool, Lindz. You don't want to look like an idiot. "Uh. Dog? No, I don't. Why?"

The woman swiveled to look Lindsey in the eye. Somehow, her gaze was disconcerting. She was a good three inches shorter than Lindsey but held herself very confidently, almost aggressively. "And you haven't seen it around?"

Lindsey hedged. "I doubt I'd forget a dog that big in a hurry."

"Okay, good."

"Good?" But the woman was already pushing past her into the cottage. "Hey, wait a moment, what the heck?"

"It's all right. I'm a friend. Name's Greta." The woman eyed the windows professionally, peered up the stairs and around the corner into the kitchen. "Smells good in here. You're the only one home, yeah?"

"Well, yes, apart from you." Maybe she shouldn't have admitted that, but this Greta character had caught her off guard. "Um, what's going on?"

"Oh, nothing much."

Lindsey glanced outside again, then studied the woman more closely. Greta's arms had good muscle tone, and her movements were quick and efficient. And she had supreme chutzpah for someone who'd just walked straight into someone else's house, as if Lindsey was the interloper here, not her. And it was only now that Lindsey realized the woman wasn't wearing a raincoat, despite the weather, and that she was holding her left hand in her pocket in a rather… odd way. Plus, was that a pager on her belt? Who used pagers anymore?

"Well, close the damned door, then," Greta said. "What is it they say up here? 'Put wood in t'hole.' "

"Sorry, what's this about?"

Should she close the door? Or should she run out of the house and slam it behind her to slow this possibly crazy person down, and call the cops?

Except that Lindsey's mobile was on the dining room table. And who knew what else was lurking out there in the night?

She could shout "Hey phone, emergency, call nine-nine-nine…" but would Greta let her get the words out?

Greta followed her gaze, walked to the table, and picked up Lindsey's phone. "This what you want? Look, I'm not going to hurt you. This is about Roger Cane."

"What?" *Oh, shit.* "Listen, there's nothing between us. We're just friends…"

"Save it." The woman strode back, slapped the phone into Lindsey's hand, then slammed the door and locked it. "I don't care what you've done with him. That's not what this is about."

"Or not done," Lindsey said quickly.

"Seriously, darlin', you could have been banging him for weeks and I wouldn't give a toss. He's not my boyfriend. He's… well. He used to be my boss, for a while. Until things went south. Ha."

"Boss?" Greta didn't look like she was in the hotel trade. Though that *hotel* story was looking less and less likely by the minute.

Greta sniffed. "Besides, you're not his type."

"Okay. Thanks." Oddly, that hurt. For all the strangeness of this encounter, Lindsey was a bit miffed to be dismissed like that. She glanced down at her phone, and up at Greta, who was off again, across the room and into the kitchen. "Hey!"

"That was a compliment, girlie. Trust me."

Lindsey was well into her forties, and Greta was early thirties at the most. Being called *girlie* by her was oddly ridiculous, even worse than *darlin'*. Contemptuous. Demeaning. But by the time Lindsey caught up, the woman was peering out the back window, up the hill. And, next, she turned the kitchen lights off, on, off, on again.

"What are you doing?" Stupid question. Greta was signaling. Obviously.

The hell with this. Lindsey pressed the actual "phone" icon on her phone and got an error message. "Oh."

She had zero bars on her cellular service, and no WiFi. Somehow. "My phone won't work," she said, rather stupidly.

"Yeah, I know," Greta said. "That's us. Deauther device in my pocket."

"De-what?"

"Deauthenticator. It sends packets to jam your WiFi, and the cellular too. Everyone in the streets close by is probably cursing us right now."

This was mad. Completely bonkers. "Why?"

"So you can't use your phone. Obviously. Are you always this thick?"

Lindsey's fear rose. "What do you want?"

"It also disables any WiFi security cameras you may have in here, or in the street."

"There aren't any."

"You might think so. You'd be surprised the tricky stuff landlords do. Now, sit *down*."

The sense of menace radiating from Greta was growing by the second. Lindsey was surprised she hadn't detected it while the woman was still standing in the street. "Who is *us*?"

"Well, that's the big question, innit?" Greta picked up the kettle. "Cup of tea, yeah? I'm parched."

Lindsey made a break for it. Shoved off from the wall and sprinted toward the front door.

It was pure instinct. Even as she ran, Lindsey knew she didn't have a prayer of twisting the key to unlock it before crazy Greta caught her.

She didn't even make it that far. Lindsey was only halfway across the hall when the kettle slammed into the back of her head. She saw stars, and stumbled, but that hardly mattered because in the next instant Greta kicked her legs out from under her.

Lindsey fell, skidded and crashed into the wall. She knocked a painting off the wall, and a vase on the console table by the front door toppled off and exploded into a mess of china shards.

Lindsey's arm was bleeding, and the breath was knocked out of her. Her phone had flown out of her hand and bounced off the door. Great. Now it probably wouldn't work even if she could get Crazy Greta to turn off the jamming device. "Ow, damn," she said inadequately.

Greta's hand appeared in front of her eyes, holding something long and thin, matt black. "See this handle?" Greta moved her thumb, and a five-inch steel blade shot out of the end. "Hey, look what it does. Shiny."

Switchblade. Flick knife. One hundred percent illegal in the UK.

Lindsey was trapped in her house with a psycho. She started to shake. "For God's sake. What do you *want*?"

Greta's voice hardened. "I want you to stop with all this crap and clean up this mess. Quick like a bunny."

Everything about Greta was incongruous. "Look, if it's money you're after—"

"Get up!" Greta shouted. "Clear the mess! Now!"

"Okay, okay, okay…"

Her unwelcome guest stepped across the kitchen and opened the cupboard under the sink. "Hey, lucky guess." She picked up the dustpan and brush and threw them at Lindsey. "Now. Do as you're damned well told."

Lindsey hurried to sweep up the debris.

Greta sighed. "Listen. Calm down, all right? Believe it or not, you're safer in here than you are out there, right now."

A likely story. None of this made sense. Lindsey tried not to stammer with her fear. "Because of… the dog?" No, that was stupid. "Except you only mentioned a dog so you could get inside."

"No, I mentioned the dog to check it wasn't yours. To make sure you didn't have it in here. I didn't think so, but…" Greta gestured with the switchblade. "Big bastard, too. Been prowling around this neighborhood for days. One night it even slept across your doorway. Scary-looking brute. You want to be careful out there."

"Thanks." Greta's words might have been touching if she hadn't said them with a sardonic, almost sneering air.

"Okay, now? Sit down, right here in this chair. Stretch your legs out. Rest them on this other chair."

Making it super hard for Lindsey to leap to her feet in a hurry. She did it.

"Now, do you want that tea or don't you?"

"Yes, please," Lindsey said meekly.

Greta fixed her a cuppa, just like a normal person might, then pulled down Lindsey's bottle of Glenfiddich from the top shelf and added a tot to each cup. But before she let go of the saucer, she fixed Lindsey with a look. "I'm being nice now, right? Aren't I nice? But, fair warning. If you throw this tea at me, I *will* cut you. D'you understand?"

"Yes." Lindsey didn't want to throw it. She wanted to drink it. She took a big gulp and burned her mouth, but the acrid tang of the whisky helped a little.

She began to reach out slowly to her left, checking Greta's face as she did so. "Landline is dead too, right?"

"Yeah," Greta said. "Be my guest."

Lindsey picked up the receiver. Sure enough, the line was silent. "And that's what the van is doing at the end of the road."

"Yeah."

"And Roger is not your boss. Or your friend."

Greta grinned. "See? Now you're being smart at last. Maybe we'll get on after all. You can be reasonable, yeah?"

"I suppose so."

"Good," Greta said. "Because if you stay reasonable, I won't need to kill you."

Lindsey felt those words like rocks in the pit of her stomach. She tried not to let it show. Somehow, she needed to regain some control over this crazy situation. She met the other woman's eye, and said slowly and clearly: "No, Greta. You won't need to kill me."

"Or even mess you up." Greta gestured with the knife. "Not even a little bit."

"Right. Or mess me up."

"Smashing." Greta pressed a button. That scary sharp blade flicked back into the handle, and she put it back in her pocket.

Lindsey felt better, just to have it not visible. She took another sip of whisky tea. "You've been watching me for days, then?"

"Yup."

"Finding out where I live. Because you're after Roger Cane."

"'Roger Cane'," the woman said with some amusement. "Yeah. That guy."

"That isn't his real name?"

"Nope. You might think he's called Cane, but he's not." The woman looked at her expectantly. "But it looks like that means nothing to you?"

"What doesn't?"

"It's a joke, innit? Roger Cane's real name is Danny Knott."

"Oh," Lindsey shook her head. "If you say so."

"So, when you see it in the gangland killing news: that's your guy."

"Gangland," she said dully. And, *Danny Knott*? It wasn't the most important thing, but Lindsey somehow couldn't associate that name with Cane's face. "Roger Cane" fit him much better. "He isn't really in the hotel trade, I take it?"

"Hotels?" Greta raised her eyebrows. "Well, he might be. Wouldn't put it past him. He has a lot of irons in the fire. But listen: Mr. 'Roger Cane' is a complete bastard. Straight up."

"And you're here to… kill him?"

Greta grinned tightly. "Eventually."

Lindsey swallowed.

"Well, not me, my own self," Greta added. "I'm just the hired help. My real boss gets the honors. Your Roger Cane has led us quite the merry dance. Lots of false trails, and all. But it was only a matter of time. And hey, thanks for doing your part."

"My what?"

"You did web searches on him. You sent texts about him to some chick in Germany. And believe it or not, there aren't that many Roger

Canes in the world. Pro tip: it takes a while to build an alias and get the driving license and passport and National Insurance number and all, and you need a fixed address to be able to do that. Danny Knott has three aliases, and we've been searching for them all. But you? Not only did you use his full alias, but you also described him in the same text stream and even sent a nice picture. And once we had your number, we could track you. Hey presto! Here we are, and young Mister Danny-Roger has had his chips."

Lindsey's mouth hung agape. "You can do all that? Tap into private lines? Track my location? In England? Isn't that..."

She'd been about to say *illegal*, which was laughable. Lindsey had the feeling that Greta and her mysterious boss had walked straight past *legal* many years ago and were now in a whole new territory.

"If you have the right contacts and enough dough, sure. How do you think the coppers do it?"

Lindsey had no idea. She'd never needed to think about it.

"Wasn't all smooth sailing. Your texts to him gave us his number, but he keeps his phone switched off unless he's on WiFi. When it's not talking to the cell towers we can't locate it, and he uses VPN and spoofs his IP address and," Greta waved her hand. "Stuff. Smart stuff. Not my department. So anyway, easiest way was to go through you." Greta checked the time and glanced at the pager at her waist.

Now that pager made sense. Even Lindsey knew that pagers worked on a lower frequency band than mobile phones. Meaning that Greta's pager wasn't jammed by the de-... deauth whatever-device.

Greta stretched like a cat and slurped the last of her tea. "Okay, darlin', we've had a lovely chat and all, but time's a-ticking and our boy will be along before we know it. Ready for some straight talk?"

Lindsey nodded, exhaled. "Sure."

Greta leaned forward. "So, listen very carefully. You want to live through tonight? Cooperate. Help us do what we're gonna do anyway, and you'll get to see tomorrow. Mess us around, and..." Greta drew her fingernail across her neck and made an obscene wet squelching sound. "And it's goodnight, Lindsey Ambler, and time for your forever dirt nap."

"Oh, God." Lindsey knocked back the rest of her whisky tea.

"Here's how this works. Cane knocks on the door. You open it, play the good hostess, charming as all get-out. Bring him in. You *do not* tip him off that we're here. You get him sat down at the dining table, where he'll have a job getting up in a hurry. Me and the boys will take care of the rest. Simple, eh?"

"The rest," Lindsey said, dully.

"We'll even leave a calling card on his body, after. That's a gang thing. So everyone will know *you* didn't do it."

Lindsey shook her head. "Why would you do that?"

"Because we *want* people to know we killed him, innit? So the next 'Roger Cane' who breaks the rules will think twice. Rubbing out Danny Knott says: cross us, and you can run but you can't hide. Not even in frigging Yorkshire." Greta shivered. "Seriously? Knott was on the run, but you? You came to Yorkshire of your own free will? Good grief. Awful place. Wet and boring."

Lindsey squelched the bizarre urge to defend the Dales. *Eye on the ball, Lindz.*

Greta glanced at her pager again. "So. Ten minutes from now I'll be letting my mates in through the back door, with their artillery." She looked around at the room layout. "Maybe one of them goes upstairs on the landing, another in the loo. Maybe one waits outside the back door. Dunno, up to them. Me, I'm hiding in the kitchen the whole time, but paying close attention. I hear anything I don't like; I see you scribbling something on a piece of paper, winking Morse code or doing semaphore with your eyebrows or any other crap, warning the mark, then the deal's off. You die with him, and just as slow. Get it?"

"Yes. I get it."

"And it won't be just me watching. We'll have eyes on you from all sides."

"Okay."

"We want him sitting at the table, nice and comfy, so we can take him."

Lindsey licked her dry lips. "What then?" *You had to ask, didn't you, Lindz?*

"Then it's going to be a very long final evening for Danny Knott."

"Oh, God." Lindsey felt sick. "You're going to make me watch you *torture* him?"

"Oh, no. No, no. Mister Draken and his warboys won't want you in here puking and crying." Greta dug in her other pocket and pulled out lengths of looped black plastic. "Zip ties. Just like the coppers use. Two hundred and fifty pounds of tensile strength, so a seven-stone weakling like you won't be getting out of them too quick. We'll just shackle you up nice and neat upstairs."

Lindsey's terror was only slightly alleviated. The idea of being trussed up and helpless as a Christmas turkey didn't appeal at all. "And you'll free me at the end?"

"Nope. We'll just call it in to the cop shop once we're well clear, so they'll find you helpless and incapacitated. Matching your story, right?"

"You've thought this through," was all Lindsey could find to say.

"Well, yeah. This has worked out fine. We even have a nice washroom to clean up afterward, before we hit the road. Wet work on the high street, we're leaving blood everywhere." She looked around again, with satisfaction. "This is much better."

Lindsey couldn't help herself. "Greta? How many people have you killed? You, yourself?"

"Well, that's a rather personal question, innit? Let's just say: enough that I don't care anymore."

"And you'll really let me go? Even though I've seen your face?"

"Lots of people have seen my face, darlin'. But I change my looks a lot. Three days from now, you won't even be able to pick me out of a lineup."

"Don't bet on that," Lindsey said, and immediately wondered why she was baiting this awful, sadistic woman. "I mean, then again..."

Greta grinned. "I like you. God knows why. So please don't do anything stupid, okay? We settle our score with your boyfriend, you walk away and tell the cops everything you saw. Honestly, go ahead. You'll have a nice story to tell. Your next boyfriend will be super impressed at how cool and edgy you are."

"Or maybe he'll be afraid I'll get him killed as well."

"Not if you don't date a frigging gangster." Greta gave her an assessing look. "And don't think I'm not seeing what you're doing. Stalling. That won't work, because I'm watching the clock and my pager and Cane's still at home, probably showering extra carefully to be all pretty and sweet smelling for you."

"For God's sake, he's not my boyfriend. What the hell did he do to you anyway?"

Now, Greta's expression hardened. "Tried to screw us over, big time. Didn't follow the code. Stepped in when he should have stayed quiet and took out a major player he should have left alone. All because he wanted a larger piece of the action for himself. Action that wasn't his." Greta leaned in, her face only inches from Lindsey's. "The man he killed was Draken's brother, and my friend. So Mr. Knott-Cane has to pay, and Draken needs to send a message, one that'll be heard loud and clear. That message goes out tonight."

Lindsey swallowed. "Okay."

Greta glanced down at her pager. "Okay, here we go. Time to let the wrecking crew in. And our other team has eyes on Cane. He's walking down the main street. He'll be here in fifteen minutes, give or take."

Greta stood up, and to Lindsey's surprise, flashed her a dazzling smile. For a moment she even looked attractive. "Places, everyone! Show time!"

Chapter Ten

Lindsey sat alone in her living room, staring at her front door. If she looked the other way, toward the kitchen door, she could see a sliver of Greta's eye glinting in the warm mood lighting. It reminded her of a snake. Or a wild dog.

Pupil shape: predators have vertically elongated pupils, while prey animals usually have horizontal pupils.

This was worse than waiting for the dentist. Much worse. And when the knock at the door came, she jumped out of her skin and found herself on her feet, with no memory of standing up.

Okay, here we go. One foot in front of the other, Lindsey. Not too fast, not too slow. Act natural.

This was insane.

Was Cane really a murderer? If he was, maybe he had good reason? It was clear that Greta and her Draken boss were… terrible people. If Cane had killed one of the Drakens, maybe the guy deserved it, if they were all as messed up as Greta.

Even if Cane *was* a killer, could Lindsey really just stand by and let them take him? Do nothing, and let him die screaming? And even if they did free her afterward—which seemed unlikely, to be honest—what would it be like to live the rest of her life knowing what she'd done?

She opened the door and smiled. *We'll have eyes on you from all sides.* And from outside the front door, across the street in the fields beyond, would be the easiest side of all to keep her surveilled. "Hi!" she said. Perky. Bright. *Everything's fine. Come in and get comfy before you die.* "You're right on time."

But Cane was already looking past her, sideways up the stairs, and all around, absorbing everything in a single sweeping glance: the scuffs on the hallway wall, Lindsey's awkward stance, the kitchen door open just a crack with no light on inside—didn't people leave the light *on* in the kitchen while they were cooking?—and what else? What other clues was Cane sensing in that moment?

Lindsey felt an instant chill.

He knows.

How could he? Cane was shrewd, but he wasn't psychic. *He must have already known.* Draken's men must have given themselves away, somehow. Maybe he'd spotted them on the road?

If so, why had he come anyway?

All of this went through Lindsey's head in the fraction of a second it took Cane to complete his fast visual. She had no doubt: the tension around his eyes was obvious; his wariness blindingly apparent.

His gaze came back to her, and the wink he gave her was almost subliminal. "Give us a kiss then!" he said, his voice cheerful but his face very serious. The greeting, completely out of character. His eyes, cold.

Numb, Lindsey stepped forward and as he faked a peck to her cheek, he murmured: "Where are they?"

She pecked him back, some bizarre area of her brain noting that he did smell clean and healthy, his cheek smooth but no reek of aftershave. Lindsey hated that smell.

Yes; in an other universe, she might just have been open to taking this "friendship" further, eventually. If Cane had only been who he'd said he was.

But now, she was already muttering: "Two upstairs, at least, one in the kitchen, another out back."

Just like that, Lindsey had made her choice. *Wow.*

No matter the consequences, she couldn't be complicit in a man's mutilation and murder.

And so: *just like that*, Lindsey was a dead woman walking. She hoped that at least they'd make it quick.

"Oh, that reminds me: I brought you a prezzy," Cane said breezily, and strode across the room. It took Lindsey a couple of beats to realize he meant a *present*, a gift, and another beat to notice the long, thin black nylon bag slung over his shoulder. For yet another of those illogical microseconds she wondered whether he'd come straight from playing a round of golf.

For God's sake, Lindz. You're about to die, at least try to concentrate.

Cane ripped away what looked like a Velcro patch at the end of his bag, and a cluster of weapons tumbled onto the floor. Two shotguns with short barrels, a small club—maybe a pickax handle?—and a large knife in a sheath, that looked almost like a small sword.

"Drakens, right?" he said conversationally.

"Yes. And Greta in the kitchen."

He just nodded and snatched up one of the shotguns.

Time seemed to slow down. Lindsey could see Cane moving quickly, but she seemed to have plenty of time to think. Almost a leisurely amount, even as she stepped away from him, looking toward the kitchen, toward the stairs, toward the back door. And desperately looking for anything that might provide cover.

Cane was one step ahead of her, or maybe five. He was flipping the table that Lindsey had spent half an hour carefully setting. Cutlery, plates, the decorative but unromantic vase of wildflowers and herbs she'd arranged, placed not in between them but off to the side as if they were an afterthought. Napkins, wine glasses, everything, tossed over onto the floor in a gigantic crash and clatter, and now the table was on its side. Cane pointed, and Lindsey immediately dropped and cowered behind it.

She heard three loud beeps from the kitchen. Greta getting paged? Then the back door crashed open, and heavy footsteps thundered down the stairs.

Cane knelt beside her, behind the tabletop that now screened them from both kitchen and stairs. One of his shotguns was on his shoulder.

...Two gigantic explosions at once. Painfully loud, deafening. The first came as someone lobbed what must have been some kind of small *bomb* into the living room. She got the briefest glimpse of a beer can flying through the air, and then it exploded. Slugs of iron flew across Lindsey's living room, embedding themselves into the table and the walls around them. China and glass shattered, though Lindsey could barely hear them. Because, right next to her, the second explosion: Cane had fired.

In the confined space of her living room, both blasts were ridiculously loud. Lindsey cried out, and squirmed, pressing her palms to her ears as pain lanced through her skull.

She ended up on her back, staring up at the ceiling. Which was now perforated with long scratches, some of them with nails embedded—a variety of nails, two to six inches long—and when she looked around, the walls were likewise shredded. *Wow. Holy crap.*

She turned to look at Cane. He was still up, his shotgun trained on the kitchen. She peeked around the side of the table.

The kitchen door twitched, and Cane fired. Again with the ludicrously loud noise. Lindsey screamed and held her head again while the small calm voice at her center muttered. *Well, maybe being deaf for the rest of my life is not the worst thing that could happen tonight.*

She twisted around. The kitchen door was punctured with deep holes, splinters had flown everywhere—but she saw no sign of Greta.

A man now stood at the bottom of the stairs, hooded and dressed all in black, as if he'd magically appeared there. Cane had worked the pump action on the shotgun and he and the dark figure both fired at once, the din of the blasts so close together that Lindsey couldn't tell them apart.

The staircase man shuddered, shook, and dropped as bright red blood exploded from multiple areas on his arms and chest. Behind Cane and Lindsey, glass and china exploded.

What Lindsey didn't know about firearms could fill a book, but she'd heard of both *birdshot* and *buckshot*. Cane's shotgun cartridge had been filled with one or the other, and the guy at the foot of her stairs was now raked with what looked like a score of bloody wounds, many of them sickeningly deep.

Cane dropped the first shotgun, picked up the second.

This was a Cane new to her, a man who thought fast and moved faster. She just hoped she could keep up, in the last moments of her life. He turned to her and said something, but her ears were ringing so badly she couldn't hear. From the way his lips had moved, *Stay put,* maybe?

Sure. Lindsey wasn't planning to go anywhere.

Cane stood, stepped left, and fired. She couldn't see what he'd hit. But she saw him pick up the machete, stride purposefully across her wrecked dining room, and bring the blade slashing down. He reached forward, pulled a second man into the living room, and slashed the man again, right across the neck.

Two down, and Greta still in the kitchen.

The same thought had obviously come to Cane because he now turned toward the kitchen door, shoved it open.

Greta was right there, small in the doorway but swinging something large. Frying pan? Dutch oven? Anyway, Cane went down, his machete flying to his right. Greta jumped over his body and was past him and out of the unlocked front door, disappearing in a flash.

Lindsey was moving before she knew it: up and across the room to slam that front door and lock it.

Cane stood up calmly, as if nothing had happened. Food and destroyed crockery littered the hardwood floor. Carefully he walked through to the back of the house, closed and locked the back door, and came back out. He ripped the hoods off the two bodies. "O'Connor and Boyle," he said. Her hearing must be coming back.

"Is it over?" she cried. "Is it over?"

Cane shook his head as he squatted by his shotguns and started reloading them. "Two down, likely four or five more still out there. That would be about normal for a kill squad. And Mark Draken will be one of them. He won't give up."

Kill squad. "Okay. We call the cops?"

"How? Phones jammed. That's how I knew they were here already. Stupid of them."

"You knew? And still came?"

Cane's jaw was so rigid that it looked like it could crack at any moment. "No one messes with my friends. You're a civilian. This is out of order."

"Thanks," she said, inadequately.

"And I can't run forever. This is the third town they've followed me to. Not going to give up, are they? Time to make a stand."

In her house? Couldn't he have just kept running? *I know a pretty street in Munich with a bunch of nice rentals.*

Lindsey kept looking around and around, expecting more black-clad thugs to smash into her house — her already trashed house — at any moment. Between the nail bomb and the shotgun blasts there was already barely a square meter of wall that wasn't pitted and strafed. The TV screen had a crater in it, and most of the knick-knacks on the shelves were destroyed or laying on their sides. It was for damned sure that Lindsey wouldn't be getting her security deposit back.

"Were they telling the truth? You killed a man?"

Cane looked up at her like she was insane. "Sure. Rubbed out a piece of shit who deserved to die. Nothing sadistic, not like these guys. Just a quick double-tap to the back of the head, done and dusted, and then I was gone."

"Done and dusted…"

Now he had a loaded shotgun in each hand, and the machete at his feet. "Ever fired a gun?"

She stared. "Of course not."

Cane blew out a short breath of impatience. "Great. In that case—"

The lights went out.

Lindsey gave another little scream; she just couldn't help it. It was suddenly very dark, spooky dark, and after everything that had just happened…

"Quiet!" he hissed. His voice was coming from lower. She couldn't see him worth a damn but could tell he'd dropped back down onto one knee. "Where's the fuse box for this house? The breaker box?"

"I… have no clue."

Cane gave another hiss that sounded very much like anger, and she flinched away from him. "Pantry, garage, basement?"

"Pantry, then." The cottage didn't have a basement or garage.

"Go turn it back on."

"You're kidding," she said. Even with gunmen outside, the idea of walking alone into her pitch-dark kitchen… "Greta's gone. They must have cut the line from outside, right?"

"Inside's easier," he said. "All you need is a—look, it doesn't matter, it's a gadget she'll have put on the box, go rip it off and flip the switch and *get the goddamned power back on.*"

Get going, Lindz.

Lindsey stood. walked across the room, glass crunching beneath her shoes. "You're sure there are more coming?"

"Positive. Likely we'll get Briggs. Gun nut. Atkinson. Completely batty, to coin a phrase: he'll be up close and personal, for choice. Fletcher: uses whatever, none of it very well. Slow thinker, quick mover. Draken will be calling the shots. And you've already met Greta."

"So, five?" Even in the dark he could tell her eyes were wide. She didn't say anything else. She didn't need to.

"Six. Davey T. will be keeping watch in the getaway van and monitoring the police channels. He's nothing to worry about."

"Police?" Apparently Lindsey was limited to repeating single words now.

"Don't get your hopes up," he said. "These boys likely set up a diversion before showing up here. Arson, maybe? A five-alarm fire thirty miles away?" He shrugged. "Whatever. Some distraction that every cop in the area will run to like flies. Now shut up, I need to listen—"

He stopped and whirled, and at the same moment, Lindsey knew why. She, too, had gotten a whiff of aftershave that certainly wasn't Cane's.

And then something tripped her, pushed her over into the dirt and broken glass on the floor, and she heard the sound of grunts and the wet impact of fists.

The lights came back on.

CHAPTER ELEVEN

Cane found himself down on the floor with Fletcher holding his shoulders and all of Briggs's weight on his legs. Atkinson, his signature cricket bat on the floor next to him, was already tying Cane's arms with one of those one of those zip-tie plastic restraints and tugging it so tight that it might cut off his circulation. Cane tried to bite him, which earned him a painful blow to his mouth that loosened some teeth. Didn't matter, he'd likely never be eating again anyway. When he tried to kick upward and dislodge Briggs, Fletcher elbowed him in the gut, robbing him of enough breath that the next tie went around his ankles sweet and quick, and a second tie in the same place for good measure.

And there he was, lying on the ground, hog-tied and unable to move.

There'd been more of them upstairs than Lindsey had known about. Or they'd come in the back windows or upstairs after the power went out. Either way: he and Lindsey were toast. Just like that, it was all over.

Crap.

Smooth operation, though. He had to give them that.

Cane leaned his head forward to spit out the blood in his mouth, then raised his gaze. Greta had Lindsey Ambler up against the wall with a blade to her throat, and Lindsey's eyes were huge with shock and terror.

Cane looked away. Civilian or not, Lindsey was as good as dead.

Then Mark Draken walked in through the front door, just as if it hadn't been locked, and surveyed the room with some pleasure. "Danny-boy! Good to see you again. It's been a long time."

"Not long enough."

"Yeah, well, now we're cutting to the chase." Draken picked Cane's machete up off the floor and eyed its blade professionally. "If you get my drift. Anyway. Here goes."

Draken knelt and began to cut away Cane's clothes, down to the bare skin. Cane had seen this movie before: he knew Draken wouldn't stop until Cane was naked aside from his shorts.

And then the verbal abuse and mockery would start, with the agonizing physical abuse to follow.

Cane put the Ambler woman out of his mind and tried to summon all his courage and strength.

Lindsey watched as they trussed Cane hand and foot and cut his clothes away. He was more muscular than she'd suspected, and his body wore a surprising number of scars. Cane had not lived an easy life.

Draken looked up at Greta. "Davey?"

Greta glanced at her pager. "Davey says we're good. No undue attention outside. No fuzz, no fuss."

How could that be? Lindsey shook her head. To her, it seemed as if the nail bomb and gunshots alone must have been audible right across to the other side of the village. "You won't get away with this."

Greta looked at her in amusement. "That's it? That's all you've got?"

Draken ignored them both, his attention fully on Roger Cane. "You of all people, Danny, you know how this works." The gang boss's tone was conversational. Lindsey watched with a doomed fascination, the way she might watch a cobra on the verge of striking. "All you had to do was stay in your lane. But you just had to be the big man, had to overstep. And when Pete called you on it, you had to go after him too. And because of that, well, here we are. We're going to mess you up, Danny-boy, and by the end, you'll be *begging* to die.

"By next week, everyone will know. We'll have the pictures, and we'll be passing them around, and they're all going to see how bad it looks when a big boy like you cries."

Cane shook his head. "You never could stop talking. Don't you ever get sick of the noise of your own voice?"

"You can't provoke me," Draken said. "Can't goad me into lashing out and making this quick. That won't fly, and especially not with this toothpick." He tossed the machete aside with some distaste and reached into his coat. "Time to make you into a work of art."

Lindsey had never seen a zombie knife before, not in real life. Only in lurid tabloid stories and, once, on a TV documentary about England's inner cities.

Cane's machete had been simple: a short straight blade and a hilt. The zombie knife that now sat comfortably in Draken's hand had a wicked curve and a sadistically serrated jet-black steel blade, mounted in a garish bright green handle. It didn't look humorous. It looked wicked. Awful.

"Oh, Jesus Christ." Lindsey tried to squirm away, but Greta held her firm.

"Tonight's the night, Danny," Draken said. "Tonight, you learn what *consequences* are."

Cane swore at him, some of the darkest profanities Lindsey had ever heard in a single sentence.

"Very brave. Let's see how mouthy you are twenty minutes from now." Draken scored Cane's bare chest with the sharp point of the knife, and Cane thrashed and gave a sour growl of pain.

"Stop it," Lindsey said. "Please. For the love of God. Just stop."

Draken looked up as if surprised to see Lindsey still there. His eyes flickered right to look at Greta. "This one. She betrayed us, yeah?"

"Yeppers," Greta said. "And right away. First chance she got."

Draken's eyes bored into Lindsey's. "Really? You stupid cow. You too: all *you* had to do was not screw up. Stay in *your* lane. But no. You thought you'd be a hero." Draken shook his head, glanced back at Greta. "Whatever. Kill her."

Greta nodded calmly. "Fast or slow?"

"You choose. I'm busy. Don't make too much noise." Draken turned back to Cane and studied him, as if wondering where to cut next.

"No!" Lindsey said and twisted to look Greta in the eye. "You promised. Roger already knew you were here. There was nothing I could have done to—"

Greta rabbit-punched her under the jaw, so quickly that Lindsey didn't see it coming. She bit her tongue, and her mouth filled with the coppery taste of blood.

"Sorry, darlin'. Nothing personal." Greta's banter was light, but the darkness behind her eyes was terrifying.

Lindsey fought, but Greta was a hell of a lot stronger than she looked. Then she punched Lindsey again, a single quick bop to her nose that sent her head cracking back against the wall.

The dual shock and pain dazed her. But that was nothing, compared to the pain around her throat as Greta looped a garrote of thin piano wire around her neck and pulled it tight. Suffocation, that's how

Lindsey would go... She tried to struggle again, but she felt dazed, as if she was underwater. Couldn't breathe...

For an insane moment she thought it was the blood roaring in her ears, or some late reaction to the deafness from the shotguns...

But no, this was a real roar, and the next moment, a giant black beast with glowing red eyes came crashing through the front window of the cottage.

Barghest, Lindsey thought.

Chapter Twelve

The beast was over three feet tall at the shoulder and longer in proportion than a real dog would have been, and it was shaggy, hugely shaggy. But it was not the creature's coat that drew the eyes first, but those thick, wide claws that now skated across the hardwood floors, leaving deep gouges before the animal braked to a stop. Next it was the great jaws, lined with thick, sharp teeth, in that long snout, and finally the blazing red eyes of the beast, bright with rage. The barghest appeared to fill the room.

Greta looked around at the sudden smashing sound and froze at the sight before her. The piano-wire garotte loosened around Lindsey's neck and she gasped, sucking air in through a raw throat that still felt constricted. She rocked forward and her hands landed on Greta's shoulders; had she not done so, she would surely have slid down to the ground.

Men of action, Briggs and Draken reacted far more swiftly, with Atkinson not far behind. Briggs raised his shotgun and fired, and again the crashing noise of the blast slammed into Lindsey's ears, ratcheting up her sick headache to a new level.

Buckshot raked the barghest's body, its multiple points of impact evident from the way its fur flew. The creature skidded and howled, its roar of pain almost as loud as the shotgun discharge.

From the floor in front of it, Draken leaned back, swinging the zombie knife, and the serrated blade raked across the barghest's left foreleg.

Uncanny as the beast was, it was still living flesh and blood. Quite a lot of blood, as it turned out.

Lindsey tried to shove Greta away, but the smaller woman seemed to regain her senses. She raised her knee to pin Lindsey back against the wall and jerked again at the ends of the piano wire.

At Lindsey's strangled scream, quickly choked off, the barghest sprang again. Its mighty jaws clamped onto Greta's midsection, and now it was the psychopath's moment to scream. The beast's momentum carried them both across the room, away from Lindsey, leaving her swaying against the wall.

Draken was already striding forward, his zombie knife in his left hand and Cane's machete in his right. Briggs had pumped his shotgun and was ready to fire again but could not do so without risking shooting his own boss.

Meanwhile, Atkinson stepped up and swung the cricket bat at Lindsey, instinctively identifying her as the cause of the barghest's rage. Lindsey dropped, and the bat slammed into the wall above her.

The barghest ripped at Greta's stomach, its jaws coming away bloody. It surged forward again and knocked Briggs aside, its claws raking his neck in passing, and came straight for Atkinson.

Atkinson jumped aside and swung again, and the cricket bat impacted the barghest's skull with a sick cracking sound. The beast crashed down, rolling over and over before fetching up against the front door.

On the floor, Roger Cane reached forward. Clumsily, he picked up a shotgun one-handed and fired. Atkinson caught the blast full in the back and slumped to the ground.

Draken slashed at Cane where he lay and then stepped up, both blades raised, to confront the barghest.

And Lindsey jumped up at him, her fingernails reaching for his eyes. She missed but raked bloody lines in his cheeks. He dropped the machete and punched her down.

Then, Draken swung the zombie knife at the great beast's throat.

The barghest had long become numb to human pain and suffering. He had been witness to many wars, battles, and even brawls over the centuries: some with bows and arrows, some with spears, some occasionally with those dangerous boom-sticks that could shatter a body and leave it broken and dying.

Usually, the barghest steered clear. Nothing good could come of being swept up in human conflicts. No reason to be anywhere near them.

Some, though, were different.

For some humans, impending death had its own smell. The humans in question clearly did not know this, or they might have tried to run from their fate. None did. Sometimes, the barghest felt compelled to lie across the doorways of their huts, or houses, or hotels. Mourning? Marking the occasion in advance? Or merely observing?

Such it had been for the man whose life was a lie, whom the other men were hunting. He would meet his death in this house, if he had not done so already.

And once in a while, perhaps once in a lifetime, there were humans whom the barghest felt a compulsion to protect. That, too, was in their aroma. He had an ancient sense of fealty to them, impossible to analyze. Like no other humans, he felt those with that particular ancestral smell as his kith, valuable beyond all other men and women. They stood out prominently in the barghest's scent-map of his world, and he could detect them over very long distances. The man in York, hundreds of years ago, had been one such, and at his most recent awakening, he had wandered far across the moors and dales before identifying this woman as another.

The basis for that fealty was lost in the mist of time. The barghest had only the vaguest images of where those compulsions originated, glimmers from the past, but when they came, he obeyed them.

Tonight, that compulsion might be the death of him.

The barghest did understand death, in his way: an ending to movement, to life. He had killed enough in his time to be familiar with what remained of his victims, and just enough awareness to be able to image himself suffering such a fate.

The green serrated blade was coming for him, the barghest could see that clearly, but the blow to his head and the multiple wounds all over his body made him sluggish to respond.

Then the woman, his kith, scooped up the other blade, the simpler and straighter weapon that this man had just dropped, and stabbed the man in the thigh with it. The man snarled with anger and pain and squirmed away.

The barghest shook his head to try to clear it. The movement brought only agony, but at least he had his power of movement back. He made to spring again… but now his kith was standing in between him and the blade man, and both still had the long knives in their hands…

Draken grinned at her, his mouth obscenely bloody. "You won't do that. Nice lady like you? You wouldn't have the balls."

He didn't know her at all.

Lindsey swung the machete with all the power she could. He jerked up his stupid evil zombie knife to try to parry her, but Lindsey's utter lack of hesitation had caught him by surprise. She might be innocent, she might even sometimes be nice, but right now her attack was as instinctive and ruthless as the barghest's.

Her machete blade sliced deep into Draken's chest. It wasn't a killing stroke; she could see that immediately. But it didn't have to be. The intense pain it brought slowed his reaction long enough for her to jump away from him.

Draken fell forward onto his knees, eyes blazing almost as red as the barghest's… and then the barghest itself scrabbled on the floor with its claws, managed to get purchase, and scooted forward to clamp its bone-crunching jaws around Draken's neck.

Lindsey looked away, but clearly heard the grinding sound as the barghest's teeth severed Draken's spine.

All of a sudden, it became very quiet. Quiet, except for the sound of the barghest feeding.

Lindsey sank to the floor. The hardwood was slick with blood, both human and animal, and still messy with the detritus from her dining table. She looked around.

From the corner, Greta stared at her with unseeing eyes. She was still breathing, those breaths coming in a labored shallow panting, but she had to be in shock and bleeding out. The mess the barghest's bite had made of her stomach must surely be fatal.

The others? Atkinson, Briggs, Draken, and Roger Cane: all were very obviously dead.

Lindsey was sharing her living space with seven people who were either dead or soon would be, plus a great doglike beast that was itself bleeding freely from multiple wounds, and which occasionally paused in its feasting on Draken's body to shake its head, as if trying to shake away the pain from all those wounds.

And yet Lindsey was still alive. The beast had shown no signs of attacking her, and every sign of protecting her.

Lindsey blinked. Thought was coming slowly, as if the bestial creature had occupied her head as well as her house, but it eventually occurred to her that if she could crawl over to Greta and find the jamming device and turn it off, she could call the police.

She began the long, painful crawl across the floor—and stopped. What would the cops make of the barghest? More to the point, would the barghest see the police as a threat, and attack them as well?

The barghest stared at her, its eyes like burning coals that seared straight into her brain. It had mercifully stopped its sickening chewing. Gore dripped from its jowls, and it was panting, not in short gasps but in deep rhythmic in-drawings of breath that sounded painful. Human blood soaked the beast's chest, and blood dripped from the many holes in its haunches. It half-sat, half-lay on the floor.

What would happen when the cops arrived? If they had guns, they might just riddle this beast with even more bullets. Cops in the UK normally didn't carry guns, but surely they would if they were responding to reports of gunfire?

She didn't want this weird, valiant beast to perish. Could she take the chance?

Then she heard a loud crash from upstairs, and the sudden reek of petrol and smoke.

Oh, God, what now?

More gang members outside the house? That hadn't occurred to her. It should have. Greta had specifically said some of the warboys would be outside, keeping watch. How many of them had Cane guessed there were? She couldn't remember, except that they for-sure had a getaway driver. In the van?

Her best guess: one of them had come to peer through the windows, seen the devastation and death inside, and…

Thrown a Molotov cocktail through an upstairs window.

Fine foreshadowing for the glass bottle that now came flying through the lounge window—the same window the barghest had smashed in through. A bottle with a flaming rag sticking out of its top. A bottle that shattered into a lake of reeking fire.

And another, moments later. Thick black smoke billowed through the room.

Oh, crap.

Chapter Thirteen

"We have to go," Lindsey said to the barghest.

It—*he*—showed no sign of understanding her, and merely looked confused. Had he never smelled smoke before? Or was he still dazed by the pummeling he'd taken?

He had no collar for her to seize. The best she could do was grab him by the scruff of the neck, and tug.

Up close the barghest stank, a vivid animal smell of dirt, sweat, and meat. "Come *on*," she said, and pulled with more desperation.

He reared up, resisting her, and that huge rack of teeth grazed along her forearm, drawing blood. Then that blunt head swung into her chest and knocked her away. "Jesus!"

How long before the whole house collapsed on them? Probably quite a long time. But they might be dead from smoke inhalation long before that.

If nothing else, the blaze should finally draw the emergency services to the house. How far away was the nearest fire station. This village? The next one over? Lindsey couldn't remember ever seeing one.

She peered out the front window. One quick motion, lunging out and in again, to take a quick peek at whatever might be outside in the street.

The white van was still there. And no sign yet of the cops or a fire engine, or even a curious bystander.

"Oh, come *on*," she said.

She turned and ran past the barghest to the back door, each footfall driving a sharp pain through her head. Her throat felt cut, fiery in itself, and when she put her hand up to her neck it came away bloody. She was in one hell of a state. But by now the curtains and the walls themselves seemed to be burning, and she could glimpse the sofa smoldering—weren't furnishings supposed to be fire resistant these days?

She unlocked the back door and threw it open, and could hear it when the breeze off the valley stoked the petrol fire to an even brighter blaze.

She stepped outside. "God damn it," she said. And turned back, to find the barghest right behind her.

The barghest was on the verge of attacking her again, she could tell. The smell of the human blood and sweat that covered her was maddening him. Pain and rage and adrenaline from the fight must still be coursing through the beast's veins. Lindsey might smell like kith, but she still reeked of food, of his prey.

"This is not my blood," she said. "At least, not most of it. That makes a difference, right?" She tore her blouse, wiped as much blood from her arm as possible, and reached it out to him. "This is me. I'm not your enemy. They're all dead. Now, it's just me."

One part of her realized how insane this was. Talking to a prehistoric beast, a cryptid, as if he could understand her? Offering her arm to a creature that could snap spines and rip off limbs?

But it felt like the right thing to do. The barghest had saved her, hadn't he?

Lindsey had little choice, anyway. Running from the beast might enrage him further and bring down his killing anger on her from behind.

The barghest sniffed her, and began to lick the blood away. *Wow.* Lindsey looked up at the red reflections of the blaze in the clouds, and let it happen.

Another gout of black smoke wafted through the house, carried on the Yorkshire breeze. And now, at last, she heard the faint sound of a siren in the distance.

"Come on, boy," she said. "Time for a walk."

Around the house, across the street, and no one tried to stop them. Into the fields. Across those fields. As if Lindsey were on some kind of automatic pilot, with the barghest padding along beside her, limping a little.

They came to a drystone wall and walked along it to a gate. Went through, walked a little further, and found a ditch.

Lindsey was almost out of strength and already shivering in the night chill, or maybe from the shock. She needed to... just *stop*. This would have to do.

"Hide in there. Lie down. Stay quiet." She paused. "You have no idea what I'm saying, do you?"

The barghest panted. The human's voice was pleasant enough, familiar even. He was getting nothing from her spoken words, but her face showed deep concern for him, and the tone of her voice implied that she could be trusted. The direction she was pointing made her intention clear.

Could he run? Could he escape, flee back to the wilds? The ache was there, the need to be far away from this scene of blood and destruction, but his ribs and legs were deeply wounded. The barghest intuited that he could run, certainly he *could*, and at some fraction of his usual speed — a self-image of him hobbling off into the darkness did cross his thoughts — but it would damage him even more. It would put strain on those ribs, rend that damaged leg even more deeply.

And this human smelled right. Even through the awful smoke and the tangy scent of his own blood, and the blood of all the other humans, this woman's scent now carried on through. Tarnished with many other bloods, but vivid enough for him not to snap at her and mean it.

The barghest did not truly comprehend lineage, but certainly this human belonged to the right pack. He had not been mistaken. She was one of his kith, and so he could trust her.

He mewled, a strangely piteous sound from a creature so formidable, and let her hide him.

And once he was down in the ditch, the woman got into it beside him.

Lindsey could *feel* how ancient this beast was. It could be just the comforting solidness of the animal, after the terrors of the evening; it might be the power of suggestion from reading all those online articles about prehistoric giant mammals, millions of years old... or it could be that the beast truly was ancient.

Petting this giant shaggy creature like a regular dog felt absurd, but Lindsey did not know how else to maintain a connection. She sank her fingers deep into his reeking fur, carefully avoiding the many wounds, scratched and rubbed, and felt a response that seemed like… pleasure? Unless she was imagining that too.

The hell with second-guessing everything. Lindsey didn't have that great a power of imagination. She truly was with an ancient creature of blood, violence, and vengeance, that had swept out of the night and out of deep history to protect her. And this mighty but gravely injured beast was responding to her.

"Don't die," she said. "Don't die."

A quarter mile away, smoke still poured into the night sky from her blazing cottage. Around it she could now see flashing lights of red and blue. The emergency services of Peasholme and the surrounding districts had belatedly turned out to deal with the havoc that had been taking place there. But Lindsey was not in the least inclined to abandon the barghest. She didn't even consider standing up, turning her back on the creature and trudging away across the farmer's field to somehow explain to the police and the firefighters everything that had happened at Hazel Cottage that night. The idea was absurd. Her duty was here.

"Don't die," she said.

Eventually the cool wind flowing down the Dales valley drove her to lie down even closer to the barghest's side. She put her arms across the beast as best she could, closed her eyes, and tried to synchronize her breathing to his snuffling, painful inhales, and to the slow pulse of his heart, but great waves of exhaustion flowed across her.

She could have sworn that the barghest was murmuring "Sleep, now", in the same tone as she was pleading with him not to die; that she should give up her consciousness just as he should cling tightly to life, but at this point it was all too confusing, her brain was a riot of contradictory emotions and feelings. Then they all faded, and Lindsey did not fall asleep as much as crash, plummeting forward into a deep pit of exhaustion with only two dim red lights at the bottom of that abyss to guide her.

Lindsey slept for a long while, dead to the cold and damp world around her.

And after that… she dreamed.

Chapter Fourteen

First, she dreamed of a man in York, a simple merchant in what from Lindsey's knowledge of history looked like the 1600s, being saved from a beating—and possibly worse—from a group of local street toughs. In her dream-mind's eye she clearly saw the barghest, or *a* barghest, a fearsome creature very much like her own, ripping those attackers apart just has he had done for her, earlier this evening. Saving that merchant, in what must have seemed to him to be some kind of dark and bloody miracle…

Lindsey forced herself awake, tried to blink away the terrible mental images, both from earlier this evening and that distant dream-past.

Next to her in the ditch her barghest was twitching, his eyes appearing to move beneath his eyelids.

Did such beasts dream?

Farther back, farther back…

Was he a sorcerer? He said he was, did Oswine the vagrant, whom many called the Ambler on account of his wandering the countryside far and wide. None believed it, though. Could he turn men into toads? He could not. Conjure up a love spell? Of course, but not one that worked. Could he even recommend fragrant herbs for cooking, brew a tea, set a poultice, read a fortune from the stars? Nay, none of that. He was just a vagrant, not a witch. And so men just tapped their temples as he went by, or gibbered back at him when he went into one of his earnest but inexplicable rants about wild animals no one else had ever seen, or memories he claimed to have of past lives, and his mystery wife and daughters who no one had ever met, and who knew what else.

It was bound to happen. One day, Oswine swore at the wrong men, men with ranks and swords. They knocked him down and he got up again, still spewing his nonsense, and so they beat him, breaking his ankle in the process, which surely put an end to his ambling for a while.

Into York Gaol they sent him, for witchcraft, which was a useful-enough catchall for men and women who should really be locked away for a bit. And it was just Oswine's really bad luck that this was in the reign of King Henry III of England, around 1250 AD, and the country was suffering a famine at that time.

And, guess what? Long story short: the other prisoners in the pit in the ground that passed for the communal goal in York that season, they grew as tired of Oswine's chatter as any other sensible man, and they were really very hungry.

And so they slew old Oswine. Killed him and ate him.

But that's not the end of the story, because afterward? Even as Oswine lost his life at their hands, these miscreants heard a howling, almost a roar from beyond the walls of the gaol. A sound that cut clear through the stone and shook up their bones as well.

And in the days to come, when these villains who had eaten up old Oswine either escaped or were freed, each one of them in his turn was hunted down and killed.

Killed horribly, as well, by a beast that tore out their throats and their stomachs and shattered their bones.

It was not a good way to die.

At least, that's what they say. That was the story that went around. I don't know as I give it much credence. But those were bad times, so is it surprising that men with no morals but plenty of opportunity might feast upon their own kind, and get eaten in return?

People always talk, and since this tale began with a man who thought he was a sorcerer, even though he could do no sorcery, who knows what to believe?

It's just a story, after all.

Farther back, farther back… and a complete change of scene, and of tone.

He snuffles at her hand as they walk through the forest, the barghest nuzzling at the hand of a human female. The great beast is lean and hungry, his bond with the woman complete.

The woman is a warrior. Her tunic and furs are practical, and her crude boots are tight around her feet. A sword hangs by her side. Her face is blue with woad. This is a woman of the Brigantes tribe, in the north of the isle of Britain.

Perhaps because this is Lindsey's dream, the woman looks just a little bit like her. Same build, same facial features. A little younger, and certainly much stronger. Her arms are toned with muscle, reminiscent of Greta's.

Greta… in sleep, Lindsey squirms and shies away from that shard of thought that brings Greta to mind.

…And then that image is gone, replaced by a scene of war. Soldiers in shiny helmets, ranked in tight lines, with long spears and tall shields emblazoned with red, and the woman has been joined by hundreds other of her kin, mostly men but with a sizeable proportion of women. All are dressed in a similar fashion, and unlike the Romans they face, the Brigantes all fight individually.

But none the less ferociously, for that.

And the women like this first one, the woman who reminds Lindsey of herself: those women, and the black wolf-like creatures that fight beside them, tearing out Roman throats and raking Roman chests and stomachs, carving a swath through the massed legions, are the ones causing the most damage, the bloodiest wreckage of Caesar's armies.

…The barghest sleeps across the doorway of the warrior woman's hut. Within she lies, injured in the battle. As yet she does not know whether her wounds are fatal, whether she will die of them and be swept away into the afterlife. She will have to wait and see.

Whether living or dead, whether here in Britain or on some stark eternal plain of fallen heroes, she feels confident the barghest will always be with her.

Lindsey awakens long enough to turn over. To warm the other side of her body against the barghest's hot flanks. Somehow it no longer seems strange to her, this sleeping pairing of woman and beast. And the barghest is breathing much more easily now. Is he healing from his wounds? This quickly?

Farther…
And yet back farther still…

Glimpses in the dark. Static images, almost soothing after those frenetically active dreamscapes she's already suffered through.

Very few cave paintings have ever been found in Great Britain. Those that have show only the normal stuff: outlines of human hands, perhaps created by pigments blown out through the mouth to form a reverse silhouette. Maybe a bird here, a bison there.

Yet there are some, down deep underground and not yet unearthed by modern man, that show other forms: mammoths, human stick figures, and dog-like creatures, in hunting tableaus. Once these come to light, they will be considered very crude and stylized. In particular, the "dogs" are all out of proportion: too large compared to the other figures, and their muzzles are very long, freakishly long. And perhaps the paint colors have changed, or even been enhanced somehow by chemical changes down deep in the cave system, but one dog in particular will be seen to have brightly burning eyes, redder than fire...

The barghest has a long future ahead of it.

<h1 style="text-align:center">CHAPTER FIFTEEN</h1>

A week and a half later, Lindsey Ambler stood in the Skipton town marketplace waiting for a bus. Her journey would take much of the day: she was only going forty-five miles in total, but she'd need to change buses twice, in Settle and Kirby Lonsdale. On the plus side the bus tickets were cheap, and Lindsey was in no hurry.

She had all the time in the world.

They had discharged her from the hospital after a few days. None of her wounds were deep and her life certainly wasn't in danger, but with the smoke inhalation, risk of infection, and general trauma they'd wanted to keep her under observation for a while. It was also easier to guard her in a hospital bed; the level of police security they'd initially put Lindsey under had been quite something.

In hospital, and in the week afterward, she'd been interviewed by the police at great length. She had told the absolute truth from beginning to end, much to her detriment; she could tell that the officers were highly skeptical of her story about the gigantic hound-creature with glowing eyes that had arrived on the scene to protect her — one detective inspector had even said: "So, ma'am, you claim you were rescued by the Hound of the Baskervilles?" However, it turned out that Lindsey and the now-deceased Greta were not the only inhabitants of the village who had caught sight of the beast. The local Peasholme police station had six sightings on file from various unconnected pillars of the local community over the week prior to the evisceration by fire of Hazel Cottage, and there'd been earlier reports from further afield.

Plus, of course, the severe damage to several of the bodies recovered from the smoking ruin of the cottage was hard to interpret any other way. Obviously Lindsey herself hadn't crunched through solid bone using only her own jaws.

Scotland Yard had been very aware of the Draken gang and Danny Knott. A couple of London detective inspectors, plus a third man who Lindsey guessed was from MI5, had come all the way up to Leeds to interview her once the local force had finished with her, although she could tell them little that she hadn't already told the Yorkshire police.

Without doubt, it was the biggest crime story the Peasholme village coppers had ever been involved with, the closest they'd ever come to the big-time of organized crime in the UK, and to their intense frustration they'd been ordered to keep it on the down-low; Scotland Yard kept anything to do with the London organized crime syndicates strictly under wraps.

Which was all to the good, as the London inspectors had eventually been able to assure Lindsey that her name wasn't circulating amid the London criminal fraternity. The death of Danny Knott, yes; the death of the man she'd known as Mark Draken, yes. But the cops seemed confident that Lindsey wouldn't be facing any further trouble. She was, as everyone kept telling her, a "civilian." The other gangs were more interested in moving into the void in the criminal fraternity created by Draken's death than in taking revenge for his slaying. It was apparent that he wouldn't be sadly missed.

Anyway: once they'd run out of questions, the cops had taken Lindsey's contact info and let her go on her merry way. Maybe there would be an inquest at some point, and if so, they'd be in touch. Until then, she was free to go.

So, this bus ride. Tonight, she would begin a two-night reservation at the rather splendidly named Shakespeare Inn Bed and Breakfast in Kendall, on the edge of the Lake District. From there she'd make her way west: Lake Windermere, Coniston Water, and beyond. She'd follow her nose and keep moving, hiking around lakes instead of across moors. A change was, after all, as good as a rest.

Which wasn't to say that Lindsey was calm and relaxed. Quite the reverse: she was still exhausted and very much on edge. Right now, even standing in a public place in her anonymous new coat and scarf and with a small bag over her shoulder, her nerves were jangling. And, at night, when she finally managed to drop off to sleep, her nightmares were… well, *gruesome*. Some of those dreams were definitely historical, as well as visceral. Even ten days after she last saw her barghest, Lindsey was still sharing his dreams.

Honestly, the smartest thing would have been to go visit friends and family down south and let them spoil her rotten for a while. She had a half-dozen open invitations from college friends, previous co-workers, and exes. But… returning to her former life had even less appeal now than it had before. Instead, Lindsey would keep trekking along the path she was already on. She'd travel further afield; to the Lakes for now, maybe back to the northern Dales and Moors once she'd gotten over some of the PTSD. There was always lots to see in Scotland, including a visit to a certain loch, and why not keep going north? She'd always wanted to visit Skara Brae, in the Orkneys.

As for the barghest?

At dawn the barghest had walked away from the ditch they had shared, and Lindsey had watched him go. He wasn't limping anymore, but neither was he completely robust. He hadn't made a full recovery, but he obviously wasn't dying. Lindsey was sure of that.

Meaning that he was still out there somewhere, that strange beast that had presaged the death of Roger Cane by lying across her doorstep, and then crashed in to save Lindsey from the Draken gang. For all his ferocity, the hellhound had protected her. Why had the barghest done that? Instinct? Intelligence? Lindsey had no idea. But the affinity she'd felt with him, at the end, still felt uncanny. And right.

Lindsey and the beast were linked. And if her barghest wanted to swing by and save her life again the next time she was in mortal danger, that would be just fine.

Maybe she should buy some treats, so she'd be ready.

Okay, that was funny. In no sane world could Lindsey imagine the barghest begging for treats. "Who's a good dog?" she said aloud, and the woman standing next to her in the bus queue gave her a funny look. There were no bona fide domestic Fidos anywhere to be seen. Lindsey just gave her a cheery smile, and the woman looked away quickly.

Perhaps Lindsey could be forgiven for feeling punchy. She was still alive, and not slain or dismembered or burned to death. And she absolutely and for-sure no longer cared what anyone else thought of her.

Just a fortnight ago Lindsey had been adrift, without a compass. Searching for direction, for a meaning to her life. Now, she'd found both.

She knew what few others did, and she knew it for certain: there was a deeper world, a hidden reality that most people never saw. And if a freaking *barghest* could come to her aid, Lindsey must surely be closer to those mysteries than most.

Despite the dangers, Lindsey wanted more. She would keep hunting for that deeper world. And even if she never had such an experience again, it still beat making PowerPoint slides to impress German businessmen.

She would keep her eyes wide open, and hope to get a closer glimpse into those mysteries. Whatever they might be.

Lindsey Ambler had the feeling she'd know them when she saw them.

About the Author

Alan Smale writes alternate history, historical fantasy, and hard SF. His novella of a Roman invasion of ancient America, "A Clash of Eagles", won the Sidewise Award for Alternate History, and his novels set in the same universe, *Clash of Eagles, Eagle in Exile, and Eagle and Empire* are available from Del Rey in the US and Titan Books in the UK and Europe. His "Roman baseball" collaboration with Rick Wilber, *The Wandering Warriors*, was published by WordFire Press, and *Hot Moon*, his alternate-Apollo technothriller with heart, set entirely on and around the Moon, was launched by CAEZIK SF & Fantasy in 2022, followed by sequels *Radiant Sky* and *Burning Night*.

Alan has sold over fifty pieces of short fiction to *Asimov's Science Fiction Magazine, Abyss & Apex, Realms of Fantasy* and many other magazines and original anthologies, and his short story "Gunpowder Treason" earned him a second Sidewise Award in 2022. His non-fiction essays have appeared in *Lightspeed, Journey Planet,* and *Galaxy's Edge.*

Alan grew up in Yorkshire, England, and earned degrees in Physics and Astrophysics from Oxford University. Until recently he performed astronomical research into Galactic neutron star and black hole binary systems at NASA's Goddard Space Flight Center, and served as the Director of one of NASA's big-three astrophysical data archives.

Find him online at https://www.alansmale.com, or follow him on Facebook/AlanSmale or Bluesky/@alansmale.bsky.social.

artist's rendition of the Barghest

Barghest

(Also Known as burh-ghest,
berg-geist, Bar-geist, Bahr-Geist,
Barguist, Gytrash, Padfoot,
The Grim, Shag, Trash, Striker,
Skriker, Black Dog, Wishthounds,
Cwn Annwn, Gurt Dog, Hairy
Jack, Black Shuck, Black Shug,
Trash, Guytrash, Boggard,
Langar-Hede, Beorh-Ghost,
Gabble Retchets, Lean Dog,
or Tatter-Foal.)

ORIGINS: Primarily found in the British Isles, but similar to black dog accounts throughout the world. This creature is called by many different names, primarily regional. Many of them stem from an association with ghosts, understandable since the black dog is primarily seen as an omen of ill fortune or death, frequenting graveyards or entering towns to shepherd passing souls or punish the damned. It has also been said to prey on lone travelers and livestock. Often, but not always, it is associated with hell and called a demon.

DESCRIPTION: This creature is known for its black fur, large, lamp-like eyes that glow either red or green, and formidable fangs and claws. Some report it as being the size of a pony, others as big as a bear. Since it is purported to be a shapeshifter, able to shrink or increase its size, as well as to transform its shape into a headless person that vanishes in flame, a white cat, or rabbit, such variations are understandable. It is said it can turn invisible, walk without making a sound, and pass through closed buildings. It is also known for its dreadful howl and a sound of rattling chains, which may or may not include the presence of actual chains.

Despite its great size, the Barghest runs very fast, such that a man could not outrun it. There is some discrepancy on whether or not it can cross water.

LIFE CYCLE: Unknown

HISTORY: The lore of the black dog — by whatever name it is called — is deeply ingrained in the culture of the British Isles, with many places recording incidents and encounters throughout history, from local gulleys to haunted prisons to churchyards bearing claw marks from close encounters. In many of the accounts there are particular places associated with the black dog, in others it wanders, appearing at the fated hour for some poor soul, laying across their threshold or rattling chains beneath their windows foretelling their death.

In some regions, however, the black dog — hailed as Gurt Dog or

Hairy Jack, depending on location—is benevolent, safeguarding children and protecting and guiding travelers.

In some instances the black dogs are said to be the spirits of those damned, such as Gabble Retchets—the souls of unbaptized children that haunt the churchyards—or Lean Dog—a wrongfully executed chimney sweep haunting the site of his execution.

Though few sightings of the black dog are reported in these modern times, they still continue, though folk are less likely to confess the encounter.

Until his decades-long disappearance, JW Harp was known for his trippy underground comic strip *Captain Thetan*, about a seafarer who controls reality for himself and others. This otherworldly character appeared in a dozen issues of the classic rare underground zine *Sandanista Romp*. JW has reemerged thanks largely to eSpec Books' Systema Paradoxa series. In 2023, JW started Skilletfire Studios with comic-book author Scott Eckelaert. Under the Skilletfire Studios mantle, JW has produced the graphic novel *Boylon Heights*, and the *Gimme Five Comics* series. Since its launch, *Gimme Five Comics* has included work by Artyom Topilin, Elena Cerisciola, John L. French, Keith Lansdale, and Joe R. Lansdale with more to come.

JW grew up in the seedy parts of South Carolina, which is all of it. He feels part Canadian and part Costa Rican these days. He lives in North Carolina. Please get in touch with him at jwharp@skilletfire.com.

CAPTURE THE CRYPTIDS!

Cryptid Crate is a monthly subscription box filled with various cryptozoology and paranormal-themed items to wear, display, and collect. Expect a carefully curated box filled with creeptastic pieces from indie makers and artisans pertaining to bigfoot, sasquatch, UFOs, ghosts, and other cryptid and mysterious creatures (apparel, decor, media, etc).

Now Featuring Cryptid Crate Jr.!

http://CryptidCrate.com